MW01094598

RODRICK THE BOLD

BOOK THREE OF THE MACKINTOSHES AND MCLARENS

SUZAN TISDALE

Cover design by Wicked Smart Designs

Copyright © 2018 Suzan Tisdale

ISBN: 978-1-943244-45-4

ALSO BY SUZAN TISDALE

Forever Her Champion

The Edge of Forever

Arriving in 2018:

Black Richard's Heart

The Brides of the Clan MacDougall

(A Sweet Series)

Aishlinn

Maggy (arriving 2018)

Nora (arriving 2018)

Coming Soon:

The MacAllens and Randalls

PROLOGUE

As a boy, Rodrick the Bold had loved Christmas Tide. His mum would decorate their little home with evergreens and holly. She would make special breads and sweet cakes, the scents alone enough to make a little boy's mouth water with anticipation.

On a special night, they would walk to the MacElroy keep and watch the Yule log — carved by their chief and his brothers — being lit. The chief's wife would give each of the children a small gift. The Christmas Tide of his eighth year, he was given a carving of a horse. He still had that little toy, tucked away in a small box he now kept hidden under a floorboard in the armory at the Mackintosh and McLaren keep.

He was all of nine when he lost his parents and sister to the ague. 'Twas an illness that swept through the MacElroy clan, leaving very few survivors. 'Twas the single most devastating event of his life, and one he never truly recovered from.

Rodrick spent the next few years being raised by a band of survivors — all men. They taught him how to fight, how to defend the keep, and how to be a man. These hardened men put little stock in

1

what they called *flowery words or deeds.* Not a one of them had a wife, though they might have fathered a child or two.

Every Christmas Tide since losing his family, Rodrick made one wish on the northern star. 'Twas a simple wish: he wanted a family.

Rodrick would have liked to call the cold, hardened men who raised him *family.* But again, they weren't the kind of men who cared for such things. Their sole focus was to defend the keep and what was left of its people.

Now a full-grown man nearing forty, Rodrick still made that simple wish each Christmas Tide. He still longed for a family, but now, he yearned for a wife and bairns to call his own. Even after all these years, 'twas the only thing he wanted in life — although he'd rather be gutted than admit such a thing to anyone. He was, after all, a hardened warrior.

Still, on this cold Christmas Tide night in 1357, he made that wish again. Under an inky night sky, dotted with stars, he found the star and made the wish. "I want naught more than a wife and bairns of me own. A family and home to call me own."

He was quite certain that wish would never come true, but one never knew what fate might just have in store. Even for a hardened warrior such as Rodrick the Bold.

CHAPTER ONE

R odrick the Bold was on a mission.
Either Heaven-sent or straight from hell, 'twas too early to say and too difficult to tell. Most likely 'twas coming from hell, for that was where he was certain his one-time friend was now burning for eternity. Charles McFarland had betrayed him, as well as every member of the Mackintosh and McLaren clan. An eternity spent with Satan seemed a fitting punishment for the atrocities he had committed.

A betrayer of trust and honor, Charles had come close to killing Rodrick months ago. Today, fighting torrential rain and thick mud up to his horse's knees, Rodrick was not so certain he was glad he had survived.

He blamed the dreams, as much as he blamed Charles, for his current predicament. Nay, he hadn't made a promise to the man whilst he had lived. He had made the promise to the God-awful, haunting dreams that had kept him awake for weeks now.

Dreams that made him wake up in a cold sweat, feeling exhausted and haunted. Horrifying, tormented images of his long dead friend calling out to him from the great beyond. They were always the same: Charles floating over the sea with his arms outstretched, his torso covered in blood as his guts dangled outside his body. He spoke, but not in words that Rodrick could understand. 'Twas as if Charles was trying to speak to him in a whisper over a wide chasm.

Then the lass would appear. A comely lass with hair the color of fire and eyes a shade of green he'd never seen before. A blend of emeralds and dew-covered spring grass, filled with tears of sorrow so deep he could feel it to his bones. *Her* words, he could hear like a gentle whisper in his ear: *Help me.*

So real and vivid were the dreams that he thought he might be losing his mind. He was sure as hell losing sleep. And to the very depths of his soul he knew the image was of a woman he'd never laid eyes on: Muriel McFarland, Charles's younger sister.

She was the reason Charles had betrayed everyone. She was the reason why Charles had tried to kill him, the reason for all his lies and for the turmoil begun amongst the clan.

Once Rodrick had learned the truth behind those treasonous acts, he understood why Charles had done what he had. However, what he did and what he *should* have done were two entirely different things. What Charles should have done was come to Rodrick and ask for his help. Instead, he chose what Rodrick considered the cowardly and foolish alternative. Charles sided with the enemy instead of coming to his friends.

Muriel had been taken as hostage a year ago as part of the devious scheme by the Bowie laird, Rutger, to take over the McLaren clan. As far as Rodrick knew, she was still being held on the Isle of Skye against her will, by a woman named Kathryn McCabe-MacDonald. Held for ransom as well as leverage against Charles.

And that was all he knew about the lass.

Other than what he saw in his dreams: that lovely face, those green eyes and that eerily haunting voice.

For weeks he tried to ignore the dreams in the hopes they would eventually stop. But they were relentless.

Now he was consumed with the deep sense that *someone* needed him. Aye, he could be completely wrong in that assessment. But the feeling would not go away no matter how hard he tried to push it aside.

So before dawn that morn he made a decision to leave the clan and go in search of Muriel McFarland.

With every fiber of her being, Muriel hated Fergus MacDonald.

For months now, he'd been her tormentor, abusing her beyond the limits that any woman should be forced to endure. One moment he was telling her what a worthless whore she was, only to turn around and rape her again the next.

And she hated his wife Anthara, just as vehemently. When Muriel had gone to her after the first time Fergus raped her, Anthara beat her nearly senseless. She accused her of lying, of trying to make her husband look like a monster in the hope Anthara would set Muriel free. It took days for the girl to recover.

Were she a stronger woman, she'd kill them both. Many a night she'd lain awake dreaming of how she could take their lives. *If only...*

If only she were stronger. Smarter. Braver. Then she might be able to find a way out of this house and off this bloody island. Oh, how she longed to be free again, to be back home with her brother. If he knew what was happening to her, he would be consumed with a murderous rage.

But Muriel had not heard from him in months. Of course, that did not mean he hadn't sent word. Mayhap he was unaware that Kathryn McCabe-MacDonald had sold her to Fergus? Mayhap he had no idea at all where she was currently being held prisoner. Knowing Fergus and Anthara the way she did, chances were strong that they were keeping any communications secret.

So, she was forced to work day in and day out, forced into submission to Fergus, all in order to repay debts that were not even of her own making. Debts her father had incurred, which had unfortunately transferred to her and her brother upon Donald McFarland's death. Her father had borrowed money from Kathryn McCabe-MacDonald's husband. If what she'd been told was true, he owed them one-hundred groats.

Certainly Charles was working hard to obtain her freedom. Knowing him as she did, he would not rest until she was released.

Fergus often liked to torture her by reminding her that it would take *years* before she could repay the large amount that was owed. He also liked to remind her that no man would ever want her now that she had warmed his bed. It sickened her when he spoke that way, as if she had *wanted* him to hurt her, as if she had *asked* him to rape her repeatedly.

And this day was no different. He'd caught her alone in the kitchen as she worked to prepare the evening meal. He had insulted her before forcing her over the table and lifting her skirts.

Tears streamed down her cheeks. The degradation was never-ending. She felt dirty and just as worthless as Fergus told her she was. It scared her when she realized how much hate filled her heart. It scared her even more when she realized he was right. No man was ever going to want her after learning the truth.

Ignoring the filthy words spewing from his mouth, she closed her eyes and tried to pretend she was *anywhere* but here. That she was back home and at an age where she was still young and innocent. When her parents were yet alive and healthy, vibrant people.

Or mayhap when she was a bit older and able to help bake the bread for her parent's shop in Edinburgh.

Bent over as she was, with her eyes closed and Fergus behind her, she didn't hear Anthara enter the room. Didn't hear her sharp intake of breath or her silk-slippered feet crossing over the stones.

But she felt the sudden rush of cold air as Fergus withdrew at the same moment a hard hand slapped her cheek. It stung and shook her out of her desperate reverie.

"You whore!" Anthara was seething, angry. Her chest rose and fell in rapid succession, her face red with fury. Her eyes were as wild as the summer storm raging outside.

"'Tis all her fault!" Fergus cried. "She seduced me!"

Quickly, Muriel adjusted her skirts and scurried away from the table. The rage in Anthara's eyes was unmistakable. There were many times over the past months when Muriel had feared for her life. But this afternoon? She believed she would soon be taking her last breath.

A moment later, Anthara was rushing toward her with hands outstretched, fully intent on strangling the life right out of her. Muriel backed away until she felt her bottom hit the wall next to the fireplace.

"I told ye to stay away from me husband!" Anthara hissed. "I warned ye!"

Finding her voice, Muriel stammered out, "I never wanted him to touch me! He has been raping me for months! I tried telling ye—"

Her words were cut off by another smack across her cheek. "Ye lie!"

"I tried to resist her, Anthara! But she kept beggin' me," Fergus said as he looked over his wife's shoulder. "I think she be a witch who has cast a spell upon me." He was smiling, his dark eyes sparkling with the knowledge that his wife would never believe a word that came out of Muriel's mouth.

There was nowhere to run, nowhere to hide. Cowering in the corner, she covered her head with her arms to protect herself from Anthara's fists. A moment later, Fergus joined in.

MURIEL LAY CURLED IN A BALL IN THE CORNER, ENVELOPED IN FEAR, HER heart pounding so hard she could feel the blood rushing through her ears. Just how long she had lain there she didn't know. All she knew was that she hurt. Not just her body, from where Anthara and Fergus had punched and kicked her, but all the way to her soul.

They had finally broken her.

She wanted to die.

Not so much due to the pain radiating up and down her spine, or from the blood trickling down her lips, or from the painful swollen cheeks. Nay, she wanted to die because there was no reason to live.

Fergus would never stop his assaults and Anthara would never intervene on her behalf. Muriel had no friends, no allies here. No one to protect her.

And to her very bones, she knew that Charles was never coming for her. He'd been unable to procure the funds for her release. Mayhap he believed she was better off where she was.

Heavy footfalls against the stone floor drew nearer. *My God, they be comin' back to beat me again.*

"Just cut me throat and be done with it," she whispered, doubtful anyone would listen. They were drawing too much pleasure out of beating her.

Someone tossed a rag that landed on her face. "Clean yerself up."

She did not recognize the man's voice – gravelly and deep. Cautiously, she opened her eyes, turned her head slightly, and looked up at him. From where she lay, he looked like a scraggly giant. His face was covered in dark whiskers, his greasy hair was pulled away from his face, and from his pungent smell, she could surmise it had been a good number of years since he'd bathed.

"I said to clean yerself up!" he growled. "We have a boat to catch."

―――――――――

RODRICK HAD BEEN ON SKYE FOR TWO DAYS AND WAS NOT ANY CLOSER to finding Muriel McFarland than he had been the day he arrived. He was sorely tempted to head to the public stables where he'd left his horse, catch the next ferry, and return to his clan.

Earlier that morn he had finally tracked down Kathryn McCabe-MacDonald at her home. The woman had pretended she had no earthly idea who Muriel McFarland was or what he was talking about. Irritated, he'd left the house to find a tavern where he could get good and bloody drunk.

As he was trudging down the path heading back into Portree, he began to feel as though he were being followed. Someone was in the woods that lined the path. He could hear the faint rustle of leaves and soft footfalls. Whoever it was, they were not very good at being unobtrusive.

Ever so slowly he placed a palm on the hilt of his sword. He didn't want the person in the woods to know he was aware of their presence.

Up ahead, the path forked and the woods ended. He wished then he'd brought his mount so he could make a swift exit if needed. God only knew who might be waiting for him at the branch in the road.

Surrounded by forest on both sides, he knew he was at a disadvantage. While he was never one to run from a fight, he was also not a stupid man. He was alone, at least a mile from Portree, without his steed or anyone to help him. But he wasn't called Rodrick the Bold for no reason.

He had just made the decision to attack first when the person in the woods drew closer to the road.

"M'laird!" a female voice whispered.

He spun with sword drawn, ready to do battle. He heard a slight squeak of fright in response.

"I mean ye no harm!" the woman called out to him.

"Show yerself," he ground out, itching for a fight.

Cautiously, the woman stepped forward through the thick brush. She was a stout woman of mayhap forty years, with light brown hair and fear-filled eyes. She glanced quickly back toward the house before looking at him again.

"I mean ye no harm, m'laird," she told him. "But I ken where Muriel McFarland be."

Dubious, he raised a brow as he narrowed one eye.

She sent another look back toward whence she'd come. "They sold her to Fergus and Anthara MacDonald, me laird's brother and his wife, they did. That poor girl!" She shivered and shook her head. "I heard ye talkin' to me mistress. She lied to ye, she did. Muriel was here for a few months, but then they sold her to Fergus."

She looked so sad — as well as afraid — that he had to believe what she was telling him. He took a long hard look at his surroundings. His instincts told him the woman was alone, that this was not a ruse to draw him into battle.

"I must get back afore she notices I be gone. Go to Portree, m'laird.

9

Help that poor girl. Fergus is no' to be trusted. I fear what he's already done to her."

She started to turn back into the woods.

"Wait!" he called out to her. "*Where* in Portree do I go?"

"They live no' far from the docks, in a big house. Just ask anyone there and they can tell ye, they can."

She said nothing else before disappearing back into the woods.

MURIEL DID HER BEST TO KEEP UP WITH HER CAPTOR. SHE'D LOST ONE slipper within moments of being all but dragged out of the house. The man — who had refused to tell her his name — declined to stop long enough for her to grab it. His sweaty hand clung to hers with such force she worried he'd crush her bones.

Down the crowded streets of Portree he pulled her. The rain had let up earlier and was now naught more than a heavy mist. Just enough so it clung to her brown dress, her face and hair. Anthara had refused to allow her to take anything with her, not even her own cloak. 'Twas one more slap in the face, another way for Anthara to prove she had the upper hand.

They headed south toward the docks through mud and muck. The cold mud seeped through her bare toes as well as her slipper. Soon, she could see the tall masts of several ships. As they drew nearer, with him shoving their way through the crowds, her heart cracked with each step she took.

Once, she tried pleading for someone to help her, to tell them she was being taken against her will. But the tall, smelly man yanked harder, giving her no time to beg for mercy.

Soon she smelled the salty sea air blended with the scent of fish and bodies that seemed as fond of bathing as the man pulling her along. Seagulls, osprey, and gannets flew overhead, diving down into the sea. The braver birds were trying to steal the day's catch from fishermen's boats.

Instinct warned her she was heading to her death. Right before they'd left Anthara and Fergus's home, Fergus had taken great delight in letting her know she had been sold to the ship's captain for the paltry sum of five groats. "And I was lucky to get *that* much, considering the shape ye be in," he had told her.

Oh, how she wanted to use her fingernails to scratch out his eyes! But there had been no time, no opportunity to do so.

As her heart cracked, her stomach roiled at the thought of what lay ahead. She'd not try to raise any false hope that the captain would be kind or generous. Any man who would buy a woman was not a man who could be trusted. And if her experience with Fergus was any indication of what lay in store for her on that ship...

She made a decision then. The first opportunity that presented itself, she would fling herself overboard and let the sea have her. Death was the only preferable alternative to the life she was certain she'd find on that ship.

"Hurry it up!" the smelly man called out over his shoulder. "The cap'n is lookin' forward to meetin' ye."

His grip on her wrist tightened as he pulled her along the dock, where several moored ships gently swayed to and fro. The sun played a game of hide-and-find with the clouds, the waves lapping gently against the shore and docks. Were her circumstances different, she might have found the scene peaceful. Instead, she was terrified.

Her escort made a sharp turn and began hauling her up a gangplank. She tried without success to wrench herself free from his grip. He ignored her as if she were naught more than an irritating fly.

If she could only free herself, she could fall into the water here, and never set foot aboard the rocking ship. Pretending to trip, she fell down onto the dirty board. He stopped, turned around and looked mightily peeved. Without saying a word, he lifted her up and tossed her over one shoulder, then continued up the plank.

Several men stood along the rail, all with greedy, hungry eyes that made her feel even dirtier. One of the men — with a toothless leer and beady eyes — stepped forward. He reached out and touched her shoulder as they went by. Her stomach churned with disgust and her heart thundered against her breast. A loud cheer went up, at which she closed her eyes and prayed.

Please, God, let someone help me!

RODRICK WASTED NO TIME RETURNING TO PORTREE. IF WHAT HE HAD been told was correct, then Muriel was in grave danger.

Once he entered the town, he stopped the first person he saw — an elderly man with thinning white hair and intense blue eyes — and asked where he might find the home of Fergus MacDonald.

"What do ye want with that son-of-a-whore?" the man inquired curiously before spitting on the ground.

Rodrick quashed the urge to tell him it wasn't any of his business. "Me younger sister has been stayin' with them fer a time. I have come to retrieve her."

The auld man's eyes grew wide with horror. "Why in the bloody hell would ye do that to a lass? Be she ugly?"

Rodrick thought the question rather odd. "Can ye tell me where their house be?" he asked. His frustration was growing by leaps and bounds.

The old man spit again before answering. "Up the road a piece," he answered with a nod in the general direction. "Ye'll find a big grand house with flowers linin' the path. And if I were ye, I would no' dally. Fergus MacDonald be a son-of-a-whore who will take advantage of any innocent lass."

There was no need for Rodrick to ask him what he meant by that. His gut told him that Muriel was in greater peril than he had imagined.

ON HIS WAY TO THE MACDONALD HOUSE, RODRICK STOPPED AT THE livery to have his horse saddled and at the ready. He wanted to leave as soon as he rescued Muriel and get off this bloody island. He could hear *Caderyn* snickering and kicking the stall. The beast disliked being confined as much as Rodrick and was just as stubborn. 'Twas one of the reasons he was so fond of the animal. "I'll be back fer ye soon enough," he called to the black stallion. *Caderyn* replied with a hard kick to the wall.

After paying the liveryman, Rodrick set off to find the MacDonald house. 'Twas just where and looked exactly like the auld man said it would. 'Twas the only grand house on the street with flowers lining the path. He wrapped his fist against the door.

He had to knock hard a second time before anyone came. He was met by a round, aulder woman, with hair black as pitch and even darker eyes. With a scrutinizing glare, she looked him up and down once before asking him what he wanted.

"I've come to get Muriel," he told her bluntly.

There was a flicker of fear as well as surprise in her eyes, but only a flicker. "There be no one here by that name," she told him before trying to shut the door.

He held it open with a strong forceful hand. "I *ken* she be here."

"Be gone with ye, ye big lout! I told ye, there be no one here by that name!"

He didn't believe her. "But she *was* here, aye?" he asked with a raised and hopeful brow.

She grunted once before glancing over her shoulder. A moment later she was leaning in to whisper. "Aye, but she be gone now. Check the docks."

"Why the docks?" he asked.

"The laird sold her off to a ship's captain a little while ago," she whispered before looking over her shoulder again.

His stomach tightened with dread before filling with anger. "What ship?" he demanded to know.

"Wheest!" she rebuked him. "I do no' ken what ship! I told ye all I ken. Now go!"

And with that, she shoved the door closed on him.

Furious, he felt his fingers tremble. *What the bloody hell is wrong with these people?*

He'd gone to the docks to try to find Muriel. The people there were far less willing to share any information with him. His inquiries were met with silence, or grunts to bugger off.

He hadn't yet met Fergus MacDonald, but he looked forward to that day. If his gut was right — and it usually was — the man was a bloody bastard of the highest form.

And it had to run in the family, for they all seemed quite at ease with selling people. So far today he had learned Muriel had been sold not once, but twice. Whilst he would have preferred to go back to find Fergus MacDonald and beat him until he confessed which ship's captain she'd been sold to, it might have made matters worse.

Frustrated, he found his way into a tavern to eat and rethink his strategy.

He sat at a table in a dark corner, ordered a meat pie and a cup of ale.

Mayhap I have lost me mind, he quietly mused. *Here I am, running around the Isle looking for a lass I have never met.*

He thought about the dreams. He now knew they *had* meant something. No longer could he refute that fact. Muriel was here on this island and she needed his help.

Why are ye doin' this to yerself? He had asked that question more than once in the past two days. *Riskin' yer own neck fer a lass ye've never met and fer a man who tried to kill ye.*

His quiet reflection was interrupted when a tall, slender man came rushing into the tavern, quickly making his way to the group of men at the table next to Rodrick's.

"Come lads, we have to get back to the ship," he said. There was an urgency in his voice.

"Bugger off," one of the men told him. "We do no' leave for another three days."

The tall man thumped his friend on the back of his head, which evoked a slur of curses.

"The captain says we be leavin' in the morn," he told them.

"Why the change in plans?" Another of the greasy looking men asked before taking a sip of his ale.

"Ye do no' need to ken why," the tall man replied. "Just finish up and get back to the ship."

"I ain't goin' nowhere," another man said. "At least no' until ye tell us why."

His friends agreed with nods and grunts of approval.

After a long moment, the man finally spoke. "The cap'n has bought himself a wench. Got her off some MacDonald fer five groats. And a pretty thing she is."

The name *MacDonald* caught Rodrick's ear. He knew at once he was talking about Muriel.

The men's attitudes changed dramatically at the mention of a pretty lass. No further convincing was needed. They slammed down mugs of ale, rose in rapid succession and headed for the door.

Rodrick was following right behind them.

CHAPTER TWO

E arlier that afternoon, Muriel believed she could not have been more afraid or in more danger. But she'd been proven wrong.

She'd been taken below to the captain's quarters, where she was tossed onto the bed and left alone. The door locking behind the disgusting man who'd brought her here sent fissures of fear tracing up and down her spine.

Her mind was racing in different directions. She either had to find a way out or a way to end her own life. She'd be damned if she was going to allow another man to do to her what Fergus had done. She'd not sit idly by and become a slave to anyone else.

Before she could act either way, she heard the door unlocking. Terrified, she scooted off the bed, looking for a way out.

A man entered the chamber, carrying a pitcher of water and washing cloths. He was just as vile and disgusting as the man who had brought her here.

"Cap'n Wallace has ordered ye clean yerself up," he said as he placed the items on a small table in the center of the room. "I'd no' dally, were I ye, fer he is a man of little patience."

He looked her up and down before leaving her alone. She held her breath in the hope that he'd forget to lock the door behind him.

He didn't.

THE SUN HUNG LOW IN THE SKY, CASTING THE SEA AND EVERYTHING IT touched in shades of red and orange. Torches were being lit along the docks. Soon, night would descend.

Rodrick did not want to risk waiting until nightfall to board the ship on which he was certain Muriel was being held captive.

He'd been watching from the shadows across the way for nearly half an hour. The men aboard were busy readying the ship to leave on the morrow. They called out and shouted to one another as they checked sails, masts and equipment.

'Twas a three-mast sailing vessel that could be powered by sail or oar. From Rodrick's vantage point, he could see two platforms located on either end of the ship. The tall masts creaked and groaned as the ship lolled gently from side to side. Numerous ropes ran from the top of each mast to the rails. Thick rope ladders were draped on either side, from mast to deck.

Knowing they'd not leave until daybreak, he'd returned to the public stables to retrieve *Caderyn.* The horse was happy to be out of the stall and whinnied his approval. Rodrick had left him standing in front of a tavern not far from the ship with the order to stay. *Caderyn* snickered once before shaking his head disapprovingly. There were times Rodrick swore the horse understood every word he thought.

He returned to his spot in the shadows, keeping a close eye on the sky as well as the ship. Soon, a line of men began to roll barrels aboard, followed by men carrying crates. 'Twas the perfect opportunity to make his way aboard the ship unnoticed.

Grabbing a crate from the pile on the dock, he hoisted it onto his shoulder and made his way up the gangplank. A short man with weathered skin ordered him to take it below.

Following the men in front of him, he descended the stairs and left the crate with the others. But instead of following the men back to the stairs, he slid into the shadows, pressed against the wall, and waited. As soon as he was alone, he went in search of Muriel.

He half expected to find her chained in some dark corner. His search yielded nothing in the lower part of the ship. Leaving the stores, he found a narrow corridor lined with doors. He was about to turn left, when he heard a woman scream with terror.

The sound curdled his blood before turning it hot with fury.

Muriel knew she was staring into the eyes of a madman.

Captain Seamus Wallace.

He was a tall, brutish looking man, with dark blonde hair that fell past his shoulders. His bright hazel eyes fairly glimmered with antici-pation. Without warning, he pounced on her at almost the exact moment he entered his chamber. Grabbing her about her small waist, he drew her toward him in a hard embrace. When she resisted — by clawing at his face — he shoved her onto the bed.

"I like a good fight before a good tumble," he said with a smile. "Fight all ye want, lassie. Ye'll still be mine before long."

Before she could scramble to her feet, he was on top of her. She struggled against his kisses as he hurried to push her skirts out of the way.

She was not about to give in without a struggle.

Though he was taller and bigger than she, she summoned the courage to pound her fists against his arms and shoulders. "Let me go!" she cried.

"Nay," he chuckled sinisterly. "Ye have been bought and paid fer, lass."

From somewhere deep within, she found the strength and energy to scream. It started low in her belly before climbing its way out of her throat and mouth.

He chuckled again. "That's it, lass. Scream fer me!"

Panic set in as she fought with all her might. Her fear, her pleas for mercy fell on deaf ears. If anything, they seemed to urge him on.

Suddenly, he stopped, his eyes growing wide with horrific astonishment. Muriel looked up to see a blade pressed against Seamus Wallace's throat.

A deep voice spoke then, and it was not one she recognized. "If ye try to alert yer men, I'll cut yer throat before ye can muster the courage to scream."

———

Seamus Wallace swallowed hard before giving a quick nod of his head.

"Up with ye, nice and slow."

It wasn't until the captain was on his feet that Muriel could see whom the voice belonged to.

He was taller than the captain and younger by at least a decade. He did not look like he belonged on the ship, for he appeared clean and no whiskers lined his face. A leather thong tied at his nape kept his brown hair away from his face. 'Twas his brown eyes that nearly sent her knees to knocking, for they were filled with murderous rage. She felt no relief at his actions, for she had no idea who the man was or why he was here.

He kept the dirk pointed at the captain, holding out his free hand. "Come, Muriel. I be takin' ye home."

Home? What home? She hadn't had a home in years. She lay there in stunned disbelief. How did he know her name?

When she didn't move, he chanced a quick glance her way, before turning back to the captain. "Charles has sent me fer ye."

That was all she needed to hear to get her moving. If she weren't still so terrified, she might have wept with joy. *Charles! He did no' forget about me!*

Quickly, she placed her hand in his as he gently pulled her off the bed. As soon as her feet hit the floor he realized she was just a slip of a woman. Her head, barely reaching his shoulders. As he shoved her behind him protectively she clung to his arm for dear life.

"Now, Captain, we will be leavin' yer ship and ye're goin' to lead the way."

Seamus glowered angrily at the two of them. "I paid fer her fair and square, lad. What makes ye think I will let ye leave this ship?"

Her rescuer took one step toward the captain, pinning him to the door with the blade once again pressed against his throat. "Because if ye do no' cooperate, I will kill ye. It be that simple."

His tone of voice, the way he stood so confidently, made even Muriel believe every word he spoke.

"What about the coin I paid fer her?" the captain asked.

The stranger who had come to rescue her grunted with disgust. "Consider it payment in exchange fer yer life."

The captain began to protest until the blade was pressed more firmly against his throat. "Do ye wish to die now?"

He swallowed hard again and shook his head.

"Then turn around and lead the way above. And remember, I would just as soon kill ye as look at ye."

The captain nodded once and began to slowly turn around.

Muriel swallowed the urge to squeal with delight, for she knew they were not off the ship yet.

WHEN RODRICK HAD FIRST SEEN THE LASS, HE THOUGHT HE HAD MADE A mistake. Her hair was not the fiery red he'd seen in his dreams. Nor were her eyes the color of emeralds and green grass. Nay, her hair was as gold as the sun and her eyes as blue as the deep sea.

And she was even more lovely than the image that had spoken to him in the dreams. He could see that even through the blackened eye and swollen lip. He could not help but believe there were more bruises hidden beneath her torn dress.

Even if she wasn't Muriel, she was a lass in dire need of his help. 'Twasn't until he mentioned Charles that he *knew* she was in fact, Muriel McFarland. He could see the relief in her eyes.

As the captain led the way to the top of the ship, Muriel clung to Rodrick's arm with a deathlike grip. He could feel her trembling with fear, could hear her rapid breaths as she followed close behind him.

As much as he wanted to kill the man in front of him, he worried more for Muriel's safety. If he gave in to the urge to slice the captain's throat, they could very well be found out before they left the ship.

He kept a tight hold on the captain's tunic as they took the ladder up. Once they were all three out of the darkness, Rodrick scanned the large open space. The gangplank was ahead and to their left.

Rodrick gave him a slight shove forward, his dirk pressed against the captain's back. They hadn't taken two steps before someone noticed them. 'Twas the same man who had ordered Rodrick to take the crate below earlier.

"Everythin' all right, Cap'n?" the man asked, concern etched on his brow.

The captain did not immediately answer, so Rodrick pressed his dirk more firmly into his back. "All is well, Domnall," he replied dryly as he took a step forward.

Just what gave them away, Rodrick didn't know, nor did he care. The man gave a loud shout to his mates. "Protect the captain!"

Soon, the deck was swarming with armed men, hell bent on protecting their captain as well as on prohibiting Rodrick and Muriel's escape.

Thinking quickly, Rodrick pulled the captain against his chest and placed the dirk against his throat. "Back!" he shouted to the approaching men. "Back! Or I swear I'll gut yer beloved *cap'n!*"

His words stopped the dozen men swarming toward him dead in their tracks. They were eyeing their captain, as well as Rodrick, undoubtedly trying to come up with a plan of action. 'Twas evident they could see in his eyes that his threat was no idle one; he was ready to act. Each of them took a step back.

Keeping his breath steady, Rodrick looked for another means of escape, in case his first plan to walk down the gangplank failed. He could feel Muriel behind him, her hands still firmly clinging to his cloak. Her breaths were ragged, filled with fear and uncertainty.

To his left was the gangplank; to his right were the stairs that led up to a platform anchoring one of tall masts. Under that platform were the stairs that took them below. He knew that if he retreated below from whence they'd just come, it would mean their inevitable deaths.

"Back, I say!" he shouted again as one of the men tried advancing.

Captain Seamus Wallace decided then to act in a most brave manner. Or foolish, depending on whom one might ask. "Kill them! Kill them both!" he shouted as he tried twisting his body around in Rodrick's tight hold.

The men lunged forward, but not fast enough. Rodrick gave a hard shove against the captain's back, which sent him hurling forward. As he collapsed against his men, Rodrick grabbed Muriel's hand and pulled her up the stairs to the platform. For the briefest moment, he thought of jumping off and into the cold water. But there was no time to ask Muriel if she could swim, and chances were they'd be caught or dead before they could reach the shore.

"Up the mast!" he told her. Placing his dirk betwixt his teeth, he lifted her by the waist and shoved her up so that she could climb the mast. Thankfully, she did not argue or otherwise protest. Like a cat climbing a tree, up she went.

He'd just grabbed the lowest rung when he felt the hilt of a dirk come down hard on his neck. Spinning quickly, with deft precision, he grabbed his own dirk and sliced the throat of the attacker. The man fell as blood spurted from the gaping wound.

Rodrick sent him tumbling back toward three men who were standing behind their comrade. A moment later, he was scurrying up the mast and catching up to Muriel. Her feet had tangled in her skirts, but she was quick to hang on and right herself.

Once they reached the top of the mast, with men clambering up after them, he unsheathed his sword, removed the belt and wrapped it around his wrist twice. Taking the end, he flung it over one of the ropes. "Hold on!" he told Muriel. She draped her arms around his neck without uttering a word.

With her clutching him tightly, he grabbed the end of his belt, wrapped it around his other hand, and gave her a nod. "Do no' let go!"

Most of their pursuers were still climbing when he jumped. Down the rope they slid, with Muriel clinging to him with all her might. Rodrick clamped his dirk betwixt his teeth and held onto his sword.

They were halfway down when he let out a shrill whistle, not an easy feat considering the dirk betwixt his teeth. But he managed the whistle: a signal for *Caderyn* to come at once.

As soon as they were near the plank, Rodrick let go. They landed hard on the deck, just a few steps from the gangplank. The fall forced Muriel to let go. He landed on his back; she landed on his front.

Rolling her off, he jumped to his feet, helped her to hers, and shoved his dirk into her hands. Two men with swords drawn were advancing toward them. With Muriel behind him, he braced his feet apart and readied himself for a quick battle.

The first man charged forward and was met with Rodrick's sword plunging into his belly. As his attacker fell, Rodrick withdrew his sword quickly and sliced the chest of the second man.

"Run!" he shouted over his shoulder to Muriel. "I will be right behind ye!"

She did not wait for him to tell her again. As fast as she could, she ran down the plank toward the dock.

With his heart pounding against his chest, he quickly subdued two more attackers before making his own escape down the plank. Muriel was heading in the wrong direction.

And *Caderyn* was not waiting for them.

RODRICK COULD HEAR THE THUNDER OF HEAVY FOOTSTEPS MAKING their way down the plank in fast pursuit. He soon reached Muriel and grabbed her hand. She squealed once until she realized 'twas he and not one of the men chasing after them.

"This way!" he shouted as he pulled her off the main street and into a dark alley.

"Wheest!" he whispered loudly as he pressed his back to the wall. When Muriel didn't move, he took her about the waist with his free hand and gently shoved her against the wall next to him.

They each held their breath as they listened to the sounds of shouts and booted feet racing down the cobblestone street.

Rodrick counted to ten before letting out his breath.

"Stay here," he whispered whilst he took a chance to look around the corner. More men were heading their way.

He pressed them farther into the darkness of the alley and they waited for the men to pass. They waited with pounding hearts and sweat-covered brows, while Rodrick planned out their next effort.

Once he felt certain no more men were coming from the ship, he took her hand in his. "We have to get to the ferry, and quickly," he told her.

Muriel nodded once, her eyes still filled with a good deal of trepidation; otherwise she didn't utter a sound.

"But first, I have to find me bloody horse!" he whispered harshly.

ONCE HE FELT CERTAIN THEY COULD LEAVE THE ALLEY, HE TOOK HER hand in his and gave it a gentle squeeze. "I'll have us off this island soon, lass."

"Who are ye?" she finally asked.

Her voice was soft and low.

"I be Rodrick," he replied as they made their way toward the dock. He whistled again, not quite as loudly, in the hope that *Caderyn* was nearby and would finally answer his call.

They passed by the tavern where he'd left his horse earlier. Candle and torchlight spilled out of the window, along with boisterous laughter. But no sign of his mount.

"Bloody damned horse," Rodrick hissed under his breath.

They came to the end of the block, where he paused to peer around the corner. He could see no signs of the men seeking them, so he pulled Muriel along. They walked swiftly toward the docks, all the while Rodrick cursed *Caderyn* for not responding.

When they came to the end of the last block, he stopped to look once again.

"Bloody hell," he cursed under his breath.

"What?" Muriel asked, looking quite fearful.

He had no desire to tell her their pursuers were waiting for them at the ferry.

The two of them had to get off this island tonight. Otherwise, there was a good chance they'd not survive until morning. The men were just as hell-bent on finding him as he was on getting off Skye.

Although he couldn't *hear* the conversation taking place between the shipmen and the ferry captain, he could tell that none of them were happy. There was much blustering and shouting and cursing taking place betwixt them.

His mind was racing for a way to get past the men and onto the ferry, when he heard the sound of a horse slowly approaching from the west. Shoving Muriel behind him, he ducked back behind the building. Though 'twas doubtful it was one of the men set on killing them, one couldn't take too many chances.

A few short moments later, the muzzle of a familiar-looking beast poked around the corner and snorted.

CHAPTER THREE

I f Rodrick hadn't been so relieved to see *Caderyn*, he would have sent him a slew of blistering curses. "Well, it be about bloody time!" he ground out as he took the reins. The animal snorted again, as if to say he didn't care how Rodrick felt about his delay.

Muriel bit her lip to keep from laughing at the duo whilst Rodrick studied the scene at the ferry dock. He knew they'd be casting off in a matter of moments. He had no desire to delay their expeditious retreat from Skye.

Two men departed the ferry, looking upset that they hadn't caught their prey. One of them threw his hands in the air and shook his head. To which the captain said something, most likely along the lines of *I told ye so.*

Soon, one of the captain's mates was pulling up the gangplank whilst another was loosening the heavy rope that moored the ferry to the dock.

"Lass, we will be leavin' now," Rodrick said as he lifted her onto *Caderyn's* back. Climbing up behind her, he clicked his tongue to urge *Caderyn* forward. A moment later, they were racing down the street, heading toward the ferry.

Their pursuers stood in wide-eyed amazement when they saw

Rodrick approaching at a full run. They waved their hands in the air and shouted, hoping to unsettle the horse. They could not have known *Caderyn* was a well-trained war-horse.

The gangplank had been withdrawn, the ferry unmoored; it was now being pushed away from the dock.

They would have to jump.

MURIEL SUCKED IN A DEEP BREATH AND HELD IT. THERE WAS NO TIME to point out to Rodrick that the gangplank had been removed or to beg him *not* to do what she was certain he was thinking of doing. Rodrick kicked the sides of his mount before giving out a great war cry.

As they neared the ferry at breakneck speed, she closed her eyes, sucked in another deep breath, and waited to plunge into the cold water. It seemed like her stomach fell away when they leaped into the air. She felt an eternity passed whilst they were suspended in air.

Then she felt them land on the deck of the ferry and skid to an abrupt stop.

Rodrick dismounted first, then was forced to pry her fingers away from the saddle. She'd been holding on with a deathlike grip.

"'Tis all right, lass," he told her as he forced her fingers away one at a time. "We landed safely."

Slowly, she opened one eye, then the other. Her breath came out in a great whoosh when she saw for herself they were safely aboard the ferry. As Rodrick helped her down, she saw and heard the men on the pier shouting at them and waving their fists in the air.

Rodrick handed the reins off to someone before helping her to a safer spot near the rear of the ferry. She all but collapsed to the floor amid a pile of crates and sacks of grain.

Her hands began to shake and her teeth to chatter, more from the shock of what had taken place in less than half an hour.

Rodrick soon returned and knelt beside her. "Wheest, lass," he whispered softly. "Ye be safe now."

She watched through teary eyes as he removed his cloak and draped it around her shoulders. *Safe.*

How long had it been since she'd felt truly *safe*? A year or more?

Although she tried valiantly to keep the tears from falling, 'twas an impossible task. "Thank ye," she told him through chattering teeth.

He smiled warmly and patted her shoulder.

"Does Charles wait fer me on the other side?" she asked as she wiped away tears with the back of her hand.

His smile slowly faded, replaced by a look of sadness and concern.

"Where is Charles?" she asked as her chest grew tight. From the look on his face, she *knew.*

"I be so sorry, Muriel," he said.

"Nay," she cried. "Nay!"

Rodrick drew her into his arms as she wept against his chest.

They stayed there for a long while with night falling, the clouds covering the stars in a blanket of darkness. The winds blew in, bringing with them a light rain that chilled her to her bones.

ONCE SHE HAD REGAINED SOME COMPOSURE SHE ASKED WHAT HAD happened to her brother. Rodrick was reluctant to tell her the truth. He would rather lie to her full out than let her know her brother had betrayed his clan. Deciding not all the details were necessary just yet, he gave her a half-truth.

"Our chief's wife, Rose Mackintosh, was kidnapped by the Bowies. Charles died during the attack to rescue her."

Muriel sniffed and wiped her face on the cloak. "He died fighting bravely then?" she asked for clarification's sake.

Rodrick cleared his throat once before answering. "I was no' there. I had been injured and was recovering. But I am certain he died fighting."

If she sensed he wasn't being completely truthful she made no mention of it. "How did ye ken of me? How did ye ken where to find me?"

"Before he died, he told our chief what had happened to ye, that ye had been kidnapped and were being held fer ransom."

She nodded once. "I thank ye, Rodrick, fer comin' fer me. I ken that were Charles here, he would thank ye as well."

He refused to speak about what Charles would or wouldn't do.

"Rest now, lass. 'Twill be a few hours before we reach land."

THE WAVES CRASHING AGAINST THE FERRY, THE CONSTANT HEAVING UP and down made Muriel sick to her stomach. Exhausted, bruised, and now consumed with grief at learning of her brother's death – it was all too much. Twice she had to lean over the side to vomit.

Rodrick didn't know how to truly comfort another person, for he'd kept his own heart well-guarded over the years. Still, he tried, but to no avail.

As he silently watched the lass fight with seasickness and grief, he felt deeply sorry for her. What hell and torment had she gone through these past months? What had Fergus done to her? Those were questions he wasn't certain he wanted to hear the answers to. Not because he was fearful of the truth or that he might think less of her. Nay, he was fearful he'd leave her in the first village they came to and head back to Skye to kill every last individual who had caused her harm or strife.

And there were too many people who had done both.

Most of his life had been spent around battle-hardened warriors. Men who faced death on a daily basis. Men who fought alongside him in rain, snow, or good weather. They were not the kind of people who shared any tender or gentle sides of themselves.

Therefore, he was at a complete loss about what to do or say to Muriel. He knew not what he could do to take her pain away, but take it away he would. He found himself making that silent promise halfway across the sea, as she cried and vomited and trembled from cold.

Someday, somehow, he would find a way to make her life better.

CHAPTER FOUR

On the off-chance Captain Seamus Wallace and his men might have decided to follow them, Rodrick and Muriel took off at breakneck speed as soon as they landed in Toscaig. 'Twas black as pitch, with only the stars lighting the way.

Whilst he would have preferred to find a room at an inn to allow Muriel time to dry off and get warm, he dared not chance it. He wanted to put as much land between them and the captain as possible.

Muriel rode in front of him on *Caderyn*. Though she wore Rodrick's cloak, she was still quite cold. Even after he wrapped his plaid around them and drew her in, her teeth chattered.

For hours they rode like the hounds of hell were nipping at their heels. South through open glens, dense forest, and even a few barley fields. Over hill and through streams, as fast as *Caderyn* could take them.

They stopped only once to rest, at the edge of a small forest, to stretch their legs and allow *Caderyn* a respite. Muriel stepped into the woods for a few moments of privacy. From where he stood he could hear her retching.

"Muriel?" he called out. "Are ye well?"

He heard her muffled reply. "Aye."

It was a long while before she returned, leaving him beset with concern. If they were being followed, he did not want to be caught unawares and out in the open. He knew the safest place for her was the Mackintosh and McLaren keep. Therefore, he made the decision to keep going.

Just before dawn, they reached the fishing village *Camhanaich*. If he kept going, they could be back at the Mackintosh keep by the nooning hour. He knew Muriel had tried to sleep, but 'twas next to impossible, considering the speed at which they were travelling.

Were he alone, he would have kept going or slept under a tree. But Muriel deserved better than to lie on the cold, wet ground. So, he did not believe it an extravagance when he paid two groats for a room at the only inn in *Shiel*.

Muriel said not a word when he helped her down from *Caderyn* and led her into the establishment. The dining space was quiet, save for the snoring of sleeping men passed out from partaking of too much drink the night before.

The innkeeper led them up two flights of stairs to a small room at the rear. "Sorry I do no' have anything bigger," the portly man with thinning brown hair said as he unlocked the door. "But 'twill keep the rain off ye at least."

He opened the door and stood back to allow Rodrick and Muriel entry. "Call down if ye need anythin'," he said. "But no' too loudly. Me wife will have a fit if we wake Black Andrew and Robert the Red."

Rodrick had no idea to whom he referred, neither did he care. He thanked the man before shutting the door behind him.

"Ye can have the bed," he told Muriel.

She eyed him with a good deal of dread. "Wh-where will ye sleep?"

He offered her his most sincere smile. The last thing he wanted was for her to worry that he was a threat to her safety. "I shall be right outside in the hall, guardin' the door," he explained. "Ye get out of yer damp clothes and rest now. And lock the door behind ye. Do no' open it fer anyone but me."

"I do no' have money to pay fer the room," she told him. She sounded as deflated as she was tired.

"Ye do no' need to worry over it, lass. Now, get some rest, aye?"

Tears filled her blue eyes again as she nodded. She removed the cloak and handed it to him. "I think ye will need this now more than me."

Her dress was ripped at the bodice, torn at the sleeves and hem, and covered in thick layers of mud. The image of this pretty lass with the bruised face, sprinkled with bits of mud, and the tattered dress, made his heart feel tight and constricted. What he truly wished to do was take her in his arms and promise her he would take care of her, protect her, and would never allow her to be hurt again. Promises she might not want and he might not be able to keep.

Instead, he thanked her, gave a short bow, and quit the room. He heard the soft click of the lock behind him.

***

RODRICK FELL ASLEEP SITTING UP, WITH HIS BACK AGAINST THE DOOR. When he woke a few hours later, he had a crick in his neck that made him wince when he turned his head the wrong way.

He yawned, stretched, and got to his feet. While he was tempted to knock on the door and see how Muriel was doing, he knew she did not need the interruption. The lass needed to sleep a good long while.

The image of her – battered, bruised, and road weary – popped into his mind. It was quickly followed by another, in which she wore a pretty blue gown with the Mackintosh plaid covering it. Her face was no longer bruised nor her hair in shambles. Nay, she was a stunning vision of beauty.

When he felt his heart skip a beat, he damned the renegade organ to Hades.

That kind of life is no' meant fer the likes of ye. Has God no' shown ye that time and time again?

Though he'd often wished for a quiet life with a wife and bairns, he knew that was not in his future. He was too hard, too blunt, and too much a warrior for such things. The one time he succumbed to such desires and feckless dreams was when he almost proposed to Leona

MacDowall. God had shown him almost instantly — by her standing up in the middle of the clan and volunteering to marry the Bowie — that *that* was not the life for him.

Besides, he'd seen too many men fall prey to the softness a woman offered. All he need do is take one look at Ian or Frederick Mackintosh. Never in his life had he seen two men so in love with their wives. While it didn't make either of them weak on the field of battle, it certainly made them look foolish at other times. Fawning over their women like two lovesick lads who didn't have the good sense to come in out of the rain.

And it left them prey to dangerous men.

Look at what happened to Ian when Rutger Bowie took his wife, Rose, as hostage, Rodrick thought. *It nearly killed the man.* But still, he had always longed for a home where he could spend Christmas Tide with those who cared for him

But nay, he would not fall victim to love and other such nonsense. Nay, he'd stay distant and cool, as he did in all things. He would take Muriel back to his clan where he was certain she could make a good life for herself. On her own, without him.

But first, he had to find her a new dress.

IT DIDN'T TAKE MUCH TIME FOR RODRICK TO PROCURE A DECENT GOWN for Muriel. Thankfully, the innkeeper's wife had a sister who was just about Muriel's size. He was also able to obtain a chemise, woolens, and boots that he prayed fit. Though it went against everything he believed in, he didn't haggle about the price. The lass was in need of these things, lest she catch her death from the cold, damp air. Or at least that was what he tried to convince himself of.

He'd also paid to have a bath taken to her room, and that was not an inexpensive feat. Though the innkeeper had explained how most just bathed in the room off the kitchen, Rodrick refused. Muriel had been through too much of late to subject herself to public bathing.

With the dress and other items in his arms, he bounded up the stairs two at a time. And bedamned if he wasn't humming a tune. He stopped at the door and was about to knock when he heard Muriel on the other side. It sounded like she was retching.

"Muriel?" he whispered through the door. "Are ye well?"

His question was met with more retching.

"Muriel!" he called out a bit more loudly. "Let me in, lass!"

She was probably dying. All alone in a dark room, in a strange town, without anyone there to hold her hand. *Bloody hell!* He cursed. *I should have stopped last night! But, nay! Like a fool, I insisted we keep traveling. And now she has caught her death!*

He was just preparing to break down the door when it opened.

Muriel looked awful. Her skin was pale, her eyes glassy, and her hair even more disheveled than when last he'd seen her. Concern swelled from his gut. "Lass, ye're ill."

She stepped away from the door and went to look out the tiny window without saying a word.

Rodrick placed the bundle on the end of the bed and went back to close the door. "Do ye have a fever?" he asked.

With her back to him, she gave a slow shake of her head.

"Mayhap ye should lie back down. We can stay here until ye feel better."

His suggestion was met with more silence.

Something niggled at the back of his mind. Muriel had thrown up several times on the ferry, and again, hours later, when they'd stopped to rest. And again, just moments ago.

Nay, that can no' be it, he thought. It could be she ate something that disagreed with her. Or simply the distress of everything that had happened to her of late. As far as he knew she hadn't had a bite to eat since the day before. He pushed the thoughts aside and decided 'twas time they talked.

"MURIEL," HE SAID AS HE TOOK A STEP TOWARD HER. "I BE TAKIN' YE to me clan. But if ye have family somewhere else ye would like to go to, I will take ye there." For reasons he couldn't fathom, it made him sad to think of her wanting to go somewhere other than with him.

"I have no family," she whispered, still looking out the tiny window. "I have nowhere else to go."

He knew 'twasn't right to feel relieved at hearing such a thing. The lass was all alone in this world. She'd just found out her brother was dead; she'd been sorely mistreated by too many people. He felt like the worst kind of cad for being relieved to hear she had nowhere to go, no one to call family.

Rodrick knew how that felt, to be an orphan. His family had died long ago. And ever since, he'd been wandering the land to find a replacement. 'Twasn't until he came to the Mackintoshes and McLarens that he finally felt like he had found a home.

"I ken ye will be welcomed amongst my clan," he told her. "They be good people."

Muriel grunted and shook her head. "I fear I no longer remember what *good people* are like."

His stomach filled with knots. "I swear to ye lass, as God is me witness, ye will never be put in harm's way again." That was one promise he knew in his heart he could keep.

He watched as she wiped away her tears with the backs of her hands. "Charles promised me, after our parents died, that he would always watch over me. He promised he would keep me safe. But he couldn't. What makes ye think ye can?"

MURIEL HADN'T MEANT TO SOUND HARSH OR UNGRATEFUL. BUT TOO much had taken place over the last year. Aye, Rodrick had rescued her from the ship and its ugly captain. But he'd come too late.

There was nothing left of the carefree girl she had once been. No longer could she smile or laugh freely. Nor could she look to her future with wonder and excitement.

Nay, she was naught more than a shell of a person. Empty inside, she no longer cared about anything. Oh, how she wanted to curl up in a corner and die. There was nothing left for her to live for.

"I do thank ye for takin' me off that ship," she told Rodrick. "But I will decline yer offer to go with ye."

"But where *will* ye go?" he asked. She heard the genuine concern in his voice but felt it misplaced. If he knew the truth, he'd most certainly walk away without so much as a backward glance. Did she deserve anything less? She certainly didn't feel she deserved anything *more.*

"Ye need no' concern yerself with it," she told him, still unable to meet his eyes.

"No' concern meself?" he asked, his voice laced with more than just a hint of shock.

"Nay, Rodrick!" she replied harshly. "Go back to yer clan." *And just let me die.*

"I bloody well will no'!" he said angrily. "I made ye a promise and it's a promise I mean to keep."

She could take no more of his honorable intentions. She spun around to face him, the tears streaming down her cheeks. "I said to leave me," she ground out.

When he took a step toward her, she winced involuntarily and shied away. A flood of memories she wished with all her heart she could make go away, flashed before her eyes.

His stern expression changed immediately, replaced with concern. "I mean ye no harm, lass."

"Ye do no' understand, and I do no' think ye ever could," she told him.

He studied her in silence for a long while. "They hurt ye." 'Twas a statement not a question.

Aye, they hurt me. But she couldn't quite admit it aloud.

The silence betwixt them stretched on. Rodrick stepped forward again, this time more slowly. "Whose child do ye carry?"

He hadn't meant to be quite so blunt. Her eyes filled at once with sorrow and trepidation. He knew in that instant that his suspicions were correct. She was with child.

Her shoulders shook as she choked back sobs. "Does it even matter?" she asked. "I be ruined all the same!"

"Aye, it matters," he replied sternly.

"Why?" she asked, lifting her hands to cover her face.

"I need to ken who I'll be killin'," he told her.

Muriel shook her head and swallowed hard. "Ye can kill him if ye want, but it changes nothin'! He raped me, he took everything from me and left me wantin' nothin' more than to die!"

It felt like a vise had tightened around Rodrick's heart. Another suspicion confirmed. A moment later, he was pulling her into his arms. She sobbed uncontrollably against his chest. Just where he found the words he next spoke, he couldn't say. "Muriel, I ken it feels like yer life be over, but it does no' have to be that way."

"I have nothin' left to live fer," she cried. "I do no' want this babe. I do no' want to go on. Every time I close me eyes, I see Fergus's face and I want to scream and cry and retch!"

Yet another suspicion confirmed. As much as he wanted to return to Skye and run his blade through Fergus MacDonald's heart, he knew he could not do that just yet. He had to get Muriel to his clan first.

Two lost souls stood in front of a tiny window in a small room at an inn. One wishing to die, the other wanting desperately for her to live. One cried a river of tears, the other offered up whatever he could to console her.

Once Muriel had cried it all out, Rodrick gently helped her to sit on the edge of the bed. Kneeling down, he took her hands in his. "Muriel, I ken all seems lost to ye, but please ken that *I* am here fer ye. Now and always."

Sniffling, she looked into his eyes with a most curious expression. "Ye do no' think me a whore?"

"God's teeth, nay!" he exclaimed. "What happened to ye was no' of yer own choosin'. I will no' ever think ill of ye, lass."

She sniffed again, still looking uncertain. "But—"

He stopped her protests with a gentle squeeze of her hand. "Lass, 'twas against your will and your spirit. And anyone who tells ye otherwise is a fool."

Rodrick firmly believed there was a special place in hell for men like Fergus MacDonald. He looked forward to sending the son-of-a-whore there someday soon. Closing the matter for any further discussion — at least for now — he drew her attention to the new gown he had acquired for her. "The innkeeper will be bringin' up a tub fer ye shortly. Ye will feel better once ye get all the mud and muck off ye and climb into a clean dress." He placed the gown on her lap and smiled.

Muriel rubbed the soft wool with her thumbs. "I have no coin for a new gown."

"Do no' worry over it," he told her as he got to his feet.

Seeing the worry in her eyes, he told her another half-truth. "The money came from Charles," he said. "I found it amongst his belongin's. Seems only fittin' it be spent on the things ye need." He had found a few coins amongst Charles's things, but 'twas not enough to cover even half of what he'd already spent. But Muriel need not ever know that.

AFTER MURIEL BATHED, CHANGED INTO HER GOWN, AND ATE A BIT OF stew and bread, she had to admit that she did feel better. But only slightly. Her ribs still ached from where Fergus and Anthara had beaten her the day before. Though the bath did help ease some of the ache in her bones, it did nothing to help ease the ache in her heart.

She was carrying the babe of a man she loathed – a babe she did not want, for it would be a constant reminder of Fergus MacDonald. How could she keep it?

Above all things, a child needed love. Her own parents had doted on her, loved her without question or reserve. Deep in her heart she knew she could not love this babe, for she despised its father and the manner in which it had been created.

Not only was she pregnant, but her brother Charles was gone. Killed in a battle trying to save his chief's wife. God, how she missed him. Charles had been her protector and closest friend for her whole life. Even more so after their parents had died. Now she had no one, save for this odd Rodrick fellow, whom she did not know, and a babe she did not want.

Why had God forsaken her? Why had He abandoned her? What crime had she committed? There were none she could think of that would be deserving of such punishment.

They left the inn as soon as they finished their meal, and then headed for Mackintosh and McLaren lands. As they rode south, she could not help but wonder what Rodrick might be expecting from her. Why would a complete stranger risk his own life in order to save hers? The only explanation she could come up with was that Rodrick and Charles had been the best of friends. The man had gone all the way to Skye and had fought valiantly against dozens of men, just to rescue her. That said much about his character, but the question of *why* still remained.

Muriel prayed he would not expect anything in return, at least not anything sordid and ugly, such as that she might be willing to warm his bed. Never would she allow any man to touch her as Fergus had done. Just the thought of it made her want to retch.

Unable to hold back that important question, she finally asked it. "Rodrick, why did ye come fer me?"

She could feel him grow tense as he sat behind her. "'Twas the right thing to do," he replied.

The right thing to do? There had to be more to it than that. "So ye oft go around rescuin' complete strangers?"

Rodrick chuckled slightly before answering. "No' often. But I will admit 'tis me first time rescuin' a pretty lass from a ship's captain."

Her stomach tightened at the words *pretty lass*. She didn't want him to think her pretty. She didn't want *any* man to think such. She wanted him to be repulsed by her mere presence, for that was how she saw herself now: repulsive, ugly, and unworthy.

They rode in silence for a long while, with each of them lost in their own thoughts. Her mind was a jumbled mess of worry and dread. Although she had nowhere else to go in this world, a very large part of her heart hoped the Mackintosh chief would turn her away. If he did, she would simply find a quiet bit of woods and die slowly. Though she would have preferred a much quicker death, taking her own life was out of the question. She wanted nothing more than to be reunited with her parents and brother and to put this life behind her.

CHAPTER FIVE

Rodrick met with Ian and Rose in private before bringing Muriel into the keep for formal introductions. Rodrick didn't think it possible for anyone to hate Fergus MacDonald as much as he did. But Rose proved him wrong.

"Please tell me ye gutted him and left his entrails for the scavengers?" Rose asked as she sat at the long table. For a woman as kind and gracious as Rose, she certainly possessed a desire for vengeance. 'Twas one more thing he liked about the lovely woman.

"I wish I had," Rodrick said. "But I thought it more important to get Muriel here first."

Rose gave a nod of understanding, though her lips were still pursed with anger. "We shall welcome her with open arms," she told him.

Ian's acceptance was not so readily acquired. "But can we trust her?" He asked. "She is, after all, Charles's sister."

From Rose's expression, she thought her husband's question ridiculous. "Ye can no' blame her for her brother's sins."

"Nay, I do no' blame her for what Charles did. However, I would proceed with a good deal of caution. Who kens if she be as inclined to betray someone as her brother was."

Rodrick could not fault Ian for his skepticism. Had it not been for Charles, Rose would never have been kidnapped. And Leona would never have met and subsequently married Alec Bowie. Were it not for Charles, lives would not have been lost and he wouldn't have come so close to losing his own.

"I suspect after ye meet her, ye will understand why I do no' think she be anything at all like her brother," Rodrick said before quickly adding, "She does no' ken what Charles did."

Both Ian and Rose looked at him dubiously. "What do ye mean she does no' ken?" Ian asked.

Rodrick blew out a deep breath. "The circumstances were such that it did no' seem a good idea to tell her. She kens he be dead, that he died in battle. But she does no' ken of his traitorous acts."

"Ye let her think he died a hero's death?" Rose asked incredulously.

He hadn't thought of it that way before. His primary concern had been only to keep Muriel safe.

Ian and Rose cast glances at one another before turning back to Rodrick. "Ye must tell her the truth," Ian told him. "Before someone else does."

"Aye," Rose agreed. "Although I am perfectly willin' to accept the lass, others might no' be so inclined."

That had been his concern as well. However, it mattered not. If Muriel could not find acceptance here, he would take her away and find her a home where she could live in peace.

MURIEL WAS MORE THAN JUST A BIT APPREHENSIVE AT MEETING Rodrick's chief, Ian Mackintosh. Though he was a handsome man with blonde hair and deep blue eyes, the scowl etched on his face told her that her wish to be turned away might very well come true. Whilst he scowled, his beautiful wife smiled at her warmly. Rodrick made the formal introductions before they moved on to the matter at hand.

Nervously, she stood in front of the long table whilst the man and his wife studied her closely. Her stomach twisted into knots as her fingers trembled. Oddly enough she felt comforted knowing Rodrick was standing beside her.

Ian was the first to speak. "Rodrick has told us what happened to ye these past months."

She felt her face burn with shame and lowered her gaze to the floor at her feet.

"We ken ye have had a most difficult time of it," Rose added, her voice filled with concern and warmth.

"I would like to hear from ye, in yer own words, how ye came to be on Skye," Ian said. He didn't sound nearly as kind as his wife.

Muriel closed her eyes and took in a deep breath. The last thing she wanted to do was recount all that had happened to her in the past year.

"'Tis all right," Rodrick whispered. "None here will judge ye fer anythin'."

Muriel glanced at him with much doubt. *Mayhap no' here in this room, but out there?*

"Rodrick speaks the truth," Rose told her.

She took in another deep breath and began. "A year ago, we were livin' in Edinburgh."

"We?" Ian interjected softly.

"Me brother Charles and I," she replied. "Our parents had both died the year before, so we had taken over the bakery they owned." She and Charles had worked so hard to keep the bakery going, partially to honor their parents. "About a year ago, I was alone in the bakery. Charles was out fetchin' flour. Two men came in." Her voice began to crack at the memory of that night. They'd been tall, terrifying looking men. And from the moment they crossed the threshold into the shop, she *knew*. Knew instinctively they meant to do her harm.

Muriel explained to Ian, Rose, and Rodrick what had happened after that. They had subdued her, tied her hands together, placed a hood over her head, and absconded with her.

That morning, right before Charles left, they had argued because she had given one of the street urchins a loaf of bread. *"We will never make a profit if ye keep givin' everythin' away,"* Charles had groused. That had been the last time she saw her brother.

"After that, I was taken to Skye, to Kathryn McCabe-MacDonald's home. She told me my father had borrowed a large sum of money from her before he died. I knew nothin' of such a debt," she told them. "But I was held and forced to work for them until Charles could repay our father's debt."

In comparison to Fergus and Anthara, living with Kathryn McCabe-MacDonald had seemed like a holiday. Though she had worked for Kathryn day and night, she hadn't been abused. At least not *physically.*

"How did ye end up as prisoner to the ship's captain?" 'Twas Rose who asked that question.

"A few months ago, Kathryn sold me to her brother-by-law, Fergus, and his wife, Anthara," Muriel answered bluntly. "They sold me to Seamus Wallace, the captain."

Purposefully, she left out the parts of how she had been abused, raped, and subsequently came to be carrying Fergus MacDonald's babe. She was too humiliated to admit the truth right now.

Ian turned his focus to Rodrick. "And ye went to Skye," he said. "Without notice or me permission."

Rodrick stood a bit taller. "Aye, I did."

"Would ye mind explainin' why ye did such a thing?"

Rodrick felt stuck betwixt a rock and a hard place. Why had Ian waited until now to ask such a thing? "'Twas the right thing to do."

Ian raised a brow and stared at him rather skeptically before Rose interceded. "Muriel," she said as she got to her feet and came around the table. "Ye will be welcome here." She placed a comforting hand on Muriel's shoulder. "Now, come, let us get ye settled in whilst Ian and Rodrick speak."

Puzzled, Muriel didn't move. "There is more ye need to ken," she said.

Rose simply smiled and urged her toward the exit. "Ye can tell me the rest of it whilst we walk."

MURIEL AND ROSE STOOD IN THE CENTER OF A SMALL HUT THAT WAS devoid of any furniture. "This will be yers fer as long as ye'd like," Rose told her. "We built these little places more than a year ago, when we first returned. Most of the families have built themselves cottages, so many of these remain vacant."

Muriel felt wholly uncomfortable at accepting the place as her own. "M'lady, as I have tried to tell ye, I do no' think ye will want me here. No' after ye hear the truth of my situation."

"Before ye tell me *yer* story, allow ye to tell ye one of me own," Rose replied.

Muriel was growing more frustrated by the moment. She didn't want to accept this woman's kind offer. She wanted to leave as soon as possible so she could begin the process of dying.

Rose did not wait for permission to begin her tale. "I have a sister. No' a sister by blood, but a sister of me heart. Her name be Aggie Mackintosh. Ye will get to meet her soon enough."

Sensing Rose was not going to stop until she was finished, Muriel folded her hands together and reluctantly gave the woman her full attention.

"Aggie Mackintosh be one of the strongest, finest women I have ever kent. She was strong, even at her weakest moments. Strong even when her father beat her – which he did often – even when the clan mocked and ridiculed her."

Muriel's curiosity was piqued. She had been raised by loving, caring parents and did not understand. "Why would her father beat her? And why would her own clan treat her poorly?"

Rose's smile began to fade. "Aggie was the chief's daughter. Her father, our chief, was as cruel and vile a man as ever walked the face of this earth. He treated her poorly. The clan apparently felt they had the right to do so as well." Rose shook her head in disgust and let out a slow breath before going on. "When Aggie was all of ten and three, she was raped by a man her father held in the highest regard, though fer the life of me, I do no' ken why. He was just as vile and cruel as Aggie's da."

Muriel's heart began to break for the poor woman.

"That rape resulted in a babe," Rose told her. "For nine long years, Aggie kept that secret. Only her mother knew the truth. Her mother passed the babe off as an orphan and raised him as her own until she died."

Muriel's eyes widened in stunned disbelief as she pressed her fingers to her mouth to suppress the urge to cry.

"For all those years, Aggie had to refer to Ailrig as her brother, no' her son. But she loved him fiercely. She loved him more than she loved her next breath."

Tears filled Muriel's eyes. "How could she?" she asked without thinking.

Rose's smile returned. "Because that babe was *hers*. No' her rapist's. Half of Aggie lived in that boy and that was the part she chose to focus on."

"Was she no' afraid he would end up like his da?"

Rose shook her head. "Nay, she was no'. Because she knew Ailrig would *never* ken who his blood father was."

Muriel understood the point Rose was trying to make. But that did not mean she agreed with it. Her circumstances were different than Aggie's, weren't they?

"Blessedly, Aggie met and married a most wonderful man. Ian's brother, Fredrick. They now have a daughter together and another on the way. Her son, Ailrig — he is eleven now — does no' ken the whole truth of how he came to be. All he kens is that he is loved and cared for. That be all that matters."

Muriel swiped at a tear and turned away. "I do no' want this babe," she admitted. "I ken that if I keep it, I will see its father every time I look at it."

Rose placed a hand on her shoulder. "I ken all seems lost to ye at the moment, Muriel. But time can change a person's heart."

"It will no' change mine. I do no' even want to live anymore."

Rose turned her around to look her in the eye. "Do no' say such a thing!" she exclaimed. "Ye have yer whole life ahead of ye."

"What kind of life?" she cried. "I will be stuck with a babe I do no' want. People will think me a whore fer havin' a babe and no' bein' married! I did no' ask fer this, no' any of this!"

Rose drew her in for a warm embrace. "Of course, ye did no'. But sometimes, God will give ye what ye need and no' what ye think ye want."

Muriel didn't want to listen to such things. Her heart hurt too much, and she felt as though God had forsaken her. Why should she put any belief into a kind or merciful God when He had allowed her to be raped and beaten repeatedly?

"Please, just think on what I have said fer a time." Rose patted Muriel's back. "Stay here, with us, and truly open yer heart and mind to the possibilities of what *could* be."

Muriel swallowed hard and nodded her head in agreement, even though she didn't agree at all.

"And if, when the time comes fer ye to have this babe and ye are still determined ye do no' want it, I be certain we can find her a good home."

Her. Thus far, Muriel had not thought of the babe as him or her. A daughter? A daughter she might be able to accept. But a son? Nay, she could not ever accept this babe if it was a boy.

MURIEL WAS GIVEN A PALLET AND BLANKETS BY ONE OF THE clanspeople. Someone else donated a small table and one chair. Rose assured her that soon enough they would have the tiny hut looking like a real home. Muriel truly didn't care, for she didn't plan on staying long. But she had made a promise to Rose to at least think about what she had said. Though she was quite certain it mattered not if she *thought* about things for a few days, a few weeks, or even a few years. The outcome would always be the same: she was not going to keep this babe. And she wasn't certain she'd live long enough to even give birth to it.

But a promise was a promise.

Nothing in the space was *hers*. Nay, she did not mind having used items, for she was not the kind of person who needed fancy things. 'Twas more that she felt her life was no longer her own. She had nothing left from her childhood but memories. She was sure that anything left behind after she had been kidnapped was long gone.

Everything was gone. Nothing would ever be as it once was. 'Twas a quite sobering thing to come to that realization. For months she could think of nothing but returning to Edinburgh, to the life she once had. She and Charles could possibly reopen the bakery and start over.

But when she realized she was carrying Fergus's babe, all those hopes and dreams and possibilities melted away like the last snowflake of winter in the hot spring sun.

Rodrick saw to getting her firewood for her brazier, and soon had a nice fire going. Muriel sat on the little chair, staring blankly at the flames.

"The evenin' meal is about to start," he told her. "I would verra much like to escort ye. I mean, if ye would like."

She gave a slight shake of her head. "Nay," she replied. "I be no' hungry."

"But ye have no' eaten since we left the inn this morn," he said. "Ye must eat somethin'."

When she did not respond, he let loose a heavy sigh and left the hut. Muriel was thankful for the silence and the solitude remaining in his wake.

She thought back to her earlier conversation with Rose Mackintosh. Muriel knew Rose meant well and that she was trying to get her to see that something good could come out of her situation. Before the upheaval in her life, she had always been a happy, cheerful person. She always tried to find the good in every situation and in every person. But if the last months had taught her anything, 'twas that not all people were good. And sometimes, there was no bright light to be found in the depths of darkness and despair.

Oh, how she wished she could go back to being the happy young girl she was before. All of nine and ten now, she felt as old as dirt and just as ugly.

Looking about her new home was too depressing for words. 'Twas just as empty as she felt inside.

A knock at the door broke through her depressed reverie. A fissure of fear traced up and down her spine. Then she heard the words Rodrick had given her repeatedly since meeting him; *Ye be safe now, lass. No harm will come to ye again.*

Pushing away the fear, she went to the door, but before opening it, she asked who it was.

From the other side, she heard a woman's voice. "I be Aggie Mackintosh."

For a long moment, Muriel held a silent debate in her mind betwixt telling the woman to go away or letting her in. Undoubtedly, Rose had sent her to help cheer the newcomer up. Muriel didn't want cheering up. She wanted to be left alone.

"I brought ye somethin' to eat," Aggie called through the door.

If Muriel's assessment of Rose was correct — that she was a woman with good intentions who was also a bit stubborn — there would be no getting away from either her or Aggie. Reluctantly, she gave in and opened the door.

Aggie Mackintosh was not at all how Muriel had envisioned her. Her black hair was plaited around her head, framing a delicate yet beautiful face — even though one side of it was horribly scarred. Intense, gold-brown eyes were filled with nothing but warmth and concern. In her hands was a tray covered with linen.

Muriel stood back and invited her in.

"I was no' sure what ye'd like, so I brought a bit of everythin'," Aggie said as she placed the tray on the table.

49

"Thank ye," Muriel murmured softly.

Aggie looked about the room and gave a slow shake of her head. "Och! I believe cells in gaols are better furnished than what they've given ye here!" she exclaimed. "If ever I mean to make a body depressed, I know where to bring them."

'Twas odd, but Muriel liked her instantly and could not help but giggle at her comments.

"I be Aggie Mackintosh," she said as she took a step forward. "I be verra pleased to meet ye."

"And I, ye," Muriel replied.

Aggie smiled warmly and took Muriel's hands in her own. "I shall leave ye be now, so ye can eat and get some rest. 'Twas a pleasure meetin' ye."

That was it? She wasn't going to lecture her or tell her how wonderful life could be if one only possessed the proper attitude? "Ye are no' stayin'?" Muriel asked with a quirked brow.

"Have ye no' done enough talkin' and listenin' this day?" Aggie asked with a tilt of her head.

Aye, she supposed she was tired of talking and listening. Mostly, she was just tired.

"I shall come visit ye on the morrow," Aggie said. "And we shall see what we can do to make this hut less a hut and more a home."

CHAPTER SIX

uriel's first week living amongst the Mackintoshes and McLarens was somewhat busy, even if she didn't venture out of her new home. Aggie and Rose visited her daily, and always with something new to add to her little hut. In no time, it began to look more like a home than an empty hovel. Soon, there were shelves on the wall — built by Rodrick — to hold dishes. Her pallet was replaced with a small bed, and more chairs were found and set around the table. Aggie and Rose, along with Aggie's son, Ailrig, and Rodrick were her only visitors. She did not care yet to meet anyone else. Her shame was such that it precluded her from leaving the safety of the hut.

As much as she hated to admit it, she genuinely liked Rose and Aggie. They were kind, warm, and generous. Not only with material things, but with their time as well. Aggie had even given her a new dress to wear. 'Twas a pretty green wool, lined at the hem, bodice and sleeves with bright goldenrod threads. She insisted 'twas a dress she had owned *for an age,* but Muriel didn't believe it for a moment. There was not a stain or repair to be found on it. She was more than grateful to have something else to wear.

She had met Ailrig the morning after she had arrived. He'd been every bit the gentleman, at least as much as any eleven-year-old boy could be. He had helped carry in the furniture and other things meant for Muriel's new home. He was so sweet and endearing, that 'twas impossible *not* to like him.

Rodrick visited her at least twice a day. At first, his visits were short; he only stayed long enough to bring her a tray of food, or buckets of water, or wood for her brazier. But as the days went on, he began to stay longer and longer. With each visit, it felt as though something was left unsaid betwixt them. She was too tired to inquire as to what that *something* might be.

During those visits, Muriel came to know Rodrick better. She had learned he had lost his parents and only sibling, a sister, a long time ago, to the black death. Rodrick needn't say a word for her to know the loss still affected him to this day. She, too, had lost her parents to an illness and could well understand how one never quite gets over that grief. And now that she had lost her brother, Charles, she felt very much the orphan.

She also learned that Rodrick preferred whisky over ale, but only in small amounts. *I be no' one to drink meself to stupidity,* he had told her one evening. She also learned that he had never truly felt at home until he came to live amongst the Mackintoshes and McLarens. She also learned that he preferred simple meals of meat pies or fish, savories over sweets. And she began to realize he had a good sense of humor.

They were taking a walk down by the stream one cloudy and breezy afternoon. The water rippled as if it were fighting against the slight wind that raked over it. All at once, the clouds parted and the wind died down.

"It looks as though summer has arrived," Rodrick said.

Muriel agreed with a quiet nod as she looked up at the sky. The sun felt good against her skin and she soaked up the warmth as she let her shawl fall from her shoulders. "Summer was me mum's favorite time of year", she said.

Moments later, the clouds returned, bringing with them even stronger breezes and a few raindrops.

"Och!" Rodrick said with a mischievous smile. "And now 'tis over. But it did last a wee bit longer than last year, aye?"

Just why she found it so funny, she couldn't begin to say. For the first time in months, she actually laughed. Unconstrained and uncontrollable, she laughed until her sides ached. The more she laughed, the more Rodrick smiled. There was also a bit of pride twinkling in his bright green eyes.

"'Tis good to hear ye laugh, lass," he said, still smiling.

"I must admit, it does feel good," she told him as she tucked her hand into his offered arm with a smile. From that point forward, Rodrick made it his mission to make her laugh as often as he could.

MURIEL WAS NOT JUST ILL IN THE MORNING, BUT IN THE AFTERNOONS AS well. This babe was certainly wreaking havoc on her body, making her constantly tired, even a bit irritable, and giving her a stomach that couldn't seem to hold anything down.

Both Aggie and Rose insisted that the upset stomach would eventually go away. But the being tired all the time? "That will no' go away until ye become a grandmother," Rose told her one afternoon. Aggie had to agree. "Bein' a mum is the hardest work a woman can ever do. But 'tis also the most rewardin'."

Muriel didn't want to hear about the rewards motherhood offered. She was still convinced she would not keep this babe. But neither of the women would listen to her when she mentioned it. Whenever she brought the matter up, one of them would immediately change the subject.

While she knew they meant well, that they were only trying to be encouraging in her time of despair, she hated the way they dismissed her concerns and worries. Though she truly did appreciate their companionship and kindness, this one thing grated on her nerves.

Rodrick was no better. He too would dismiss her complaints. "Ye'll feel differently after ye have the babe," he would say in a most irritatingly reassuring tone.

Betimes she wished they weren't so nice. Mayhap then she could wallow in her own misery a bit better. But 'twas growing more and more difficult to grouse and feel morose when one was surrounded by such good, kind people.

Being the people they were, they'd not pity her, nor would they help flame the fuel and add to her brooding moods. If she were honest with herself, she would admit she was glad for their positivity.

'TWAS ON THE EIGHTH DAY OF HER ARRIVAL THAT THINGS CHANGED. Muriel woke up that morning with an upset and sour stomach, which had become her normal state of being. She was also just as tired as she always was, even after going to bed early the night before.

Nay, she hadn't changed, but Rodrick had. He arrived at noontime, looking as though he were about to meet the king. His face was freshly shaved, his hair still damp from bathing, and he smelled quite nice. He wore a fresh, dark blue tunic and black leather trews. Even his boots looked clean and the hilt of his sword glistened in the sunlight.

"Good day to ye, Muriel," he said as he stood in the doorway.

"Rodrick," she said as she stepped aside to allow him in.

He didn't budge.

"What be the matter?" she asked, sensing something was amiss. Was she imagining things, or did he seem nervous?

"I would like ye to take a walk with me," he said.

She began to protest. "I do no' think—"

"Please?"

'Twas more sheer curiosity than his plea that made her grab a shawl and leave her hut.

The yard was bustling with all manner of people, mostly men who were busy working on building the keep. Women stood around fires and tables as they prepared meals. Children ran through it all without a care in the world.

And not one person gave her any notice.

54

Not one.

Mayhap they had been ordered by Rose and Ian to leave her be. Either way, she wasn't certain if she would have preferred they threw stones and insults over the silence she was met with.

Rodrick led her out of the yard, through the great wall, and away from the keep. "Where are we goin'?" she asked nervously.

"Just fer a walk, lass. We'll no' go far."

Whether 'twas instinct or the fact that Rodrick had never done anything to make her feel ill at ease, she was not filled with fear or dread. She had to admit that she did like his company. She felt safe whenever he was near.

They headed south until they came upon a wide, meandering stream. The sound of water trickling over the rocks and pebbles was relaxing. It was a beautiful day, with the sun hanging high, bathing the land in warmth and comforting brightness. Flowers in shades of pale yellow, dark pink, and lavender peeked their heads through the tall grass that waved in the gentle breeze.

They followed the stream until they came upon a copse of trees. In the distance, Muriel could hear the faint sounds of men working on the keep. The rhythmic *tap tap tap* of hammers against wood and the occasional shout of an order wafted in on the breeze.

Rodrick stopped and turned to face her. For the first time since meeting him, she actually took the time to truly look at him. He was not what some would call a handsome man. But neither was he horrible to look upon. The breeze picked up his long brown hair, making him look even more a warrior. His bright blue eyes held an intensity and warmth that didn't make sense to her at the moment.

"Muriel," he began, then his voice caught in his throat. He cleared the knot and tried again. "Muriel, there be something I want to say and ask ye."

Puzzled, she nodded and gave him permission to continue.

He started to speak, stopped, and started again. He grew frustrated rather quickly and let out a sharp, irritated breath. "God's bones," he mumbled as he raked a hand through his hair.

"Rodrick? What be the matter?" she asked, growing more and more confused.

He stared at her for a long moment before throwing his hands in the air. "I be makin' a mighty mess of things, aye?"

She had no idea what he meant by that.

Another exasperated sigh and he tried once again. "I ken we have no' known each other long, lass. And I ken I be no' the most handsome or brightest of men. But I be a good man. An honorable man who keeps his word. Ye ken?"

Not understanding what he was trying to say, she could only nod her head. "Aye, I believe ye be an honorable man."

He smiled then. A wide, happy smile. "I am," he said as he continued to look upon her with that fond smile.

"Is that all?" she said after a long moment of silence had passed.

"Nay," he finally answered. "Nay, that no' be all."

Muriel was doing her best to remain patient until he was able to tell her what was weighing so heavily on his mind. "And?" she asked, hoping to prod him into getting to the point.

"I want to marry ye," he finally blurted out.

Stunned, she took a step back, uncertain she had heard him correctly. "What?" she asked breathlessly.

"I want to marry ye."

RODRICK HAD COME TO THAT DECISION A WEEK AGO. IT HAD TAKEN HIM this long to get up the courage to ask. Finally he had decided to take the chance today, for he was fearful someone else might before he had the opportunity. That had happened once, with Leona MacDowall. With a deep sense of desperation, he did not want a repeat of that day.

He knew he had very little to offer Muriel, but he would give anything he owned to hear her say yes. Instead, she looked at him with horror-filled eyes. It did little to bolster his ego or his hopes.

"I ken I be a bit aulder than ye," he told her. By more than a decade if anyone chose to count. Nearly two if he were honest. "And I ken I be no' the most handsome man ye'll ever meet." There were countless others amongst his own clan who were far easier on the eyes than he. "And I do no' have much to offer ye," he added. "But whatever I have be yers."

Tears welled in her pretty eyes and she took another step back. "Ye can no' mean what ye're askin'," she said.

"But I do mean it, lass," he replied bluntly. He had grown to care for this young woman a great deal. 'Twas not just that she needed a husband and father for her unborn child. That was part of it, but not all of why he was asking. He found her beautiful, smart, and witty. That was when she wasn't so consumed with what had happened to her. "I—"

"Nay," she said, the look of horror still etched on her face. "Nay, I can no' marry ye. I can no' marry anyone!"

"But yer babe," Rodrick replied. "Yer babe will need a father."

'Twas mayhap not the right thing to say.

THE BABE. THE BABE! MURIEL'S LIFE NOW REVOLVED AROUND A BABE SHE did not want. Everyone seemed to be more concerned with this child who was conceived out of a violent act than they were concerned with *her*.

"I will no' marry ye, or any man," she said as she swallowed back the tears and bile. "And I am *no'* keepin' this babe! As soon as it's born, I am giving it away. I never want to see it, to look at it, or touch it, do ye understand? And I want to be left the bloody hell alone about it!"

She didn't wait for a response before turning away and fleeing, leaving him standing alone next to the stream.

Her emotions and thoughts ran rampant. Were her situation different, had she not been raped, were she not carrying Fergus MacDonald's babe, she might very well have said yes to Rodrick's proposal.

But her situation wasn't different.

It was as real as the grass she was running through. It was as real as the deep ache in her heart.

It was as real as the babe growing inside her.

She didn't want a proposal born out of pity, and that was all Rodrick's proposal was; a sheer act of pity.

Lord, she knew she was being foolish and even selfish, but she could not help it. These feelings boiling up inside her, this constant sense of despair and anguish over what had happened to her would not cease. No matter how hard she prayed to feel differently or to forget the last year of her life. There was no running from it and no way to deny it.

Through the open gates she ran straight to her hut. She slammed the door behind her and fell onto her bed. Her tears came in great, wracking sobs.

She knew she had hurt Rodrick's feelings, but that had not been her intent. She knew she owed her life to him. But to marry him out of a sense of gratitude or despair? Nay, that would not be fair to either one of them. Rodrick deserved far better than that. There was no hope for her. She was a lost soul without a future. And there was no way she could ever be a true wife to him.

Around and around her emotions went — from anger to guilt and everything in between — until her head spun and her stomach churned.

How can I make him understand? She cried silently. *How can I make anyone understand when I do no' quite understand it myself?*

RODRICK STOOD FROZEN IN PLACE AS HE WATCHED MURIEL GO.

He had never felt more dejected than he did right now. His heart cracked a little more with each step she took away from him.

Ye be a fool, Rodrick. A bloody fool.

Why he thought she would accept his proposal to begin with, he could not now imagine. Mayhap he hoped she was just desperate enough to say yes. Mayhap he thought she could overlook his shortcomings — and there were many — and agree to a union betwixt them.

Until the past year, having a wife and children was nothing more than a dream and ridiculous wish. Though he believed he didn't truly deserve those things, the yearning for hearth and home, for a wife and bairns, had grown stronger.

Mayhap 'twas because he was not getting any younger. Mayhap he was tired of roaming the country looking for a place to call *home*. He was tired of looking, tired of waiting and wishing for things that he now believed were no longer possible. He truly assumed Muriel was his last hope at having the kind of future he now yearned for.

What was wrong with him that turned women away? He was a strong man, with good morals, and held himself to a high standard of honor. He did not drink in excess, he never chased after bar wenches and whores. He could be a good provider to a family.

The more he thought on it, the angrier he became. He may not be as handsome as Ian Mackintosh, but neither was he a monster. He might not be a man of flowery words or poetry, but neither was he an idiot.

Ye be a warrior, fer the sake of Christ, he cursed under his breath. "That be all ye are, Rodrick MacElroy. A warrior."

Mayhap 'twas time to set aside this yearning for a home and accept what he was.

It did not take long for word to reach Aggie and Rose that something was amiss with Muriel. The two women came to her hut as soon as they heard. Muriel was in no mood for company. "Go away," she called from her bed. Rodrick must have told them, the traitorous man! Now they were here to try to convince her to marry him. They knocked again. "I said go away!" she shouted to the door.

The two women did not heed her demand and came in anyway.

Muriel's eyes were red and swollen from crying. Keeping her back to the door, she remained curled into a ball and holding a pillow to her chest.

"Muriel," Rose said as she came to sit on the edge of the bed. "We heard ye came through the gate cryin'. What happened?"

Mayhap they truly didn't know. "I do no' wish to talk about it."

"Och, lass!" Rose said as she patted her shoulder. "Ye must talk about it. Ye will feel better."

Anger bubbled from deep in her stomach. "Nay I will *no'* feel better. Ye will no' listen anyway. Ye'll just ignore me and tell me I will feel better *later. After* the babe is born. Everything is always *after* the babe is born with ye two!"

Rose and Aggie giggled. They *laughed* at her distress. Furious, she sat up in the bed and glared at them. "'Tis no' funny!"

Aggie brought a chair over and sat next to her. "Lass, we laugh because we have both been with child. We understand that yer feelin's, yer emotions, they sometimes do no' make a lick of sense when ye're carryin'. That 'tis why we do no' take everythin' ye say so seriously."

Appalled, she stared at them with mouth agape. "Ye think, ye *truly* think I be so upset all the time because I be with child?"

Each of them nodded *aye*.

The tears began to fall again, but not out of a sense of sadness. These were tears of sheer anger. "I be upset all the time because of Fergus MacDonald! Because he raped me. Repeatedly. Over and over again for three solid months. I be upset because I feel dirty, unworthy, used, and ugly! I be upset because every time I close me eyes I see *his* face. I *hear* his words in me sleep. *Ye be a whore, Muriel. Naught but a whore. Ye like it when I do this to ye. Admit it!*" She took in a deep breath and shook her head. "I carry the babe of a man I despise, a man I wish I had had the strength to kill. A man who torments me day and night even now."

Rose started to speak, but Muriel stopped her. "Nay! I will no' listen to ye tell me how I will feel after this babe is born. Do ye no' understand? I am no' the same happy, cheerful girl I used to be. He destroyed her. He destroyed *me*, and left *this*," she spread her arms wide as if to say *take a good long look*. "I have no future. I have no life.

All me hopes and dreams are gone now. I will never have a chance at a normal life, at a happy life. Neither of ye could ever understand that!"

Aggie quirked a brow and stood up. "Rose, will ye go and check on Ada fer me?"

Rose did no' argue. Quietly she left them alone.

ONCE THE DOOR CLOSED BEHIND HER, AGGIE LOOKED AT MURIEL. "YE think *I* do no' understand?" she asked with a raised brow. "If anyone here understands, it be me."

Immediately, Muriel felt guilty for saying no one would understand. But she truly believed her circumstance was different than Aggie's. How the woman had been able to overcome what had happened to her, she could not understand. Neither could she understand how Aggie had been able to keep, raise, and love her son.

"Think ye be the first women ever raped? Think ye the first woman who has ever gone through what ye be goin' through?"

Muriel swallowed hard before replying. "Nay," she murmured. "But—"

Rose stopped her protest. "There be no *but*. I too, have gone through what ye have. 'Tis true I was only raped once, no' repeatedly like ye. But me attacker? He left me with three things. One, this scarred face," she said, turning the scarred cheek so that Muriel could get a better look. "Secondly, he left me with child. I was only three and ten." Turning her head, she looked Muriel in the eyes. "And he left me with a sense of fear that only someone like us could ever understand."

Aggie sat down on the edge of the bed. "Muriel, I *do* understand. I ken how the fear can take over yer life. I ken how it hurts. There were many times I wished I could just die. Just close me eyes and never wake up. But God did no' answer those prayers."

"That is all I want right now," Muriel admitted. "To die. To walk away, find a quiet place, and let death come fer me."

Aggie's knowing smile said she knew all too well that feeling.

Muriel's next thought was of Ailrig. "How can ye love Ailrig as ye do?" Muriel asked.

"Because he be *mine*. Half of him is *me*. I could no more give him up than I could fly," she said as she patted Muriel's hand. "'Tis true, I did worry he would be more like his father than me, but either by God's good grace or the way I raised him, he is nothin' at all like the man who raped me."

Muriel never thought of it that way, that half this babe was made of her own blood.

"Ailrig does no' ken that I be his mother by blood. Fredrick adopted him after we were married. I do no' think I shall ever tell Ailrig the truth of it, fer I do no' want him to worry that he might turn out like the man who sired him."

"I will no' ever say a word," Muriel promised.

Aggie smiled and thanked her for keeping that confidence. "Fredrick has done much to help me. 'Twas through his love and kindness that I was able to stop bein' afraid, stop holdin' me head in shame, and to stop me stutterin'."

Muriel's brow creased. "Ye stutter?"

"No' anymore," Aggie said with a smile. "But it used to be so bad, I did no' speak fer many years."

Muriel thought that an awful thing but said nothing.

"Fredrick helped me find me voice," Aggie said as her lips curved into a warm smile.

Muriel wiped her tears on her sleeve. "Rodrick asked me to marry him," she told her.

Aggie lifted a pretty brow. "And that is what upset ye so?"

"Aye," Muriel whispered.

Aggie nodded her head as if she understood. "Ours was an arranged marriage of sorts, Fredrick's and mine. We did no' love each other at first."

Muriel stared in wide-eyed curiosity. "'Twas no' a love match?"

Aggie giggled. "The furthest thing from a love match," she said. "'Twas months before we even consummated our marriage."

Truth be told that was also a fear of Muriel's. How could she give herself freely to Rodrick? Or any man for that matter?

"Fer ten long years after I was raped, I lived in constant fear, ye ken. The fear was always with me. Fear he would come back and do it again. Fear he would learn Ailrig was his and would take him from me. Fear that me da would find out and force a marriage betwixt us." Her smile faded with thinking of those possibilities. "But something happened months after I married Fredrick. He showed me I no longer had to be afraid, ye see. And I finally decided that I had given far too many years to me rapist. I decided that I was no' going to give him any more of meself than what he took — and he took everything."

"Fredrick never insisted or demanded more?" Muriel asked.

"Nay, he did no'. He knew, ye ken, about what had happened to me. Fredrick be more than just a kind man, ye see. He be honorable and patient. Even if we had never joined as a man and wife do, he would still love me, and he would still be a good father to Ailrig."

Honorable. In her heart she knew Rodrick was an honorable man. But could he be as patient with her as Fredrick had been with Aggie?

Sensing what she was thinking, Aggie smiled warmly. "I think Rodrick be a good man, Muriel. But the only way ye'll ken if he would wait until ye are ready is to ask."

Muriel felt her face grow warm with embarrassment. "I think I hurt him too much," she said. "I screamed at him and told him nay, that I could no' marry him or any other man."

"I think Rodrick will understand. But ye must talk to him. If he is the kind of man I think he is, then he will."

Muriel was filled with doubt on that matter.

Her thoughts soon turned to her babe. Aggie was right in that half this babe was her own. Could she ignore the other half that helped make it?

"God has a plan fer ye, Muriel. I do no' ken what that plan be, but I do believe everythin' will turn out as it is meant to. Ye simply have to open yer heart to all that *could* be and no' dwell on what has been."

THE MORE RODRICK THOUGHT ON THE MATTER, THE ANGRIER HE became. He was not angry with himself or even with Muriel. Nay, he was angry with Fergus MacDonald.

He'd stayed by the stream for a long while, pacing and thinking.

Muriel had not been upset because he had proposed. She was upset because of what Fergus had done to her. 'Twas all still too raw and fresh in her mind. Roderick had been a fool for asking so soon. Had he thought it out more clearly, he would have waited to ask for Muriel's hand. Such as after he killed Fergus MacDonald and brought his head in a basket and presented it to her. Mayhap then she would realize she never had to fear the man again, nor would she have to fear Rodrick.

Rodrick was not a man to mince words or to flower them to help break a fall so to speak. Nay, they did not call him Rodrick the Bold for those reasons. He was Rodrick the Bold because he was as fierce on the battlefield as he was off it.

But he wanted her to want *him*. Not so much in the physical sense, but more in her heart. With a deep need he couldn't understand let alone try to explain, he wanted Muriel to be as fond of him as he was of her.

Without a doubt, he knew he had to apologize to Muriel. He could count on one hand the number of times he had apologized in his lifetime. And he'd still have five fingers left.

Still, he raised his head high, put his shoulders back and headed to Muriel's hut. First he would apologize for his proposal. Then he would make her a promise: he'd bring Fergus MacDonald's head to her either in a basket or on a pike. The choice was hers.

He rapped gently on the door and held his breath. As soon as she opened the door, his heart fluttered in his chest. 'Twas more than just his deep seeded need to help her, to make her feel safe. He truly liked the young woman. He also thought her quite beautiful, even though her eyes were red from crying.

Thankfully, she did not slam the door in his face. Nay, she did something quite odd considering the state she had been in an hour before. She smiled, a bright, beautiful smile and looked quite relieved to see him. "Rodrick," she said as she let him in.

Surprised, he could only stare at her in muted silence. What had caused this turn around in behavior?

She sat down at the little table and offered him a seat. "I be sorry for how I reacted earlier. I do no' want ye to think that I could no' marry *ye* in particular," she told him.

That was good to hear, and he told her so. "I, too, wish to apologize," he said. "I think mayhap me proposal was too soon. I did no' mean to hurt ye."

"Ye did no' hurt me," she replied softly. "But I ken that I hurt ye. And fer that, I be truly sorry."

Aye, her initial response had stung. But after he had thought about it, he could not fault her for her reaction. "I can assure ye, me feelin's are quite intact," he said.

They sat in silence for a time while Muriel puzzled over just how to broach the one thing weighing heavily on her mind. After Aggie left, Muriel had plenty to think about. *God has a plan fer ye,* Aggie had insisted. But just what that plan was, Muriel had no earthly idea. However, she was now quite willing to consider the possibility that she might not be meant to live all the rest of her days alone, terrified, and consumed with guilt.

"Rodrick, I have to ask ye a question. One that I find a bit embarrassin'."

Curious, he raised and brow and said, "Lass, ye can ask me anythin'. I will no' make light or fun of ye."

He watched as she took in a breath, her gaze turning to the table. "If we were to marry," she began in a soft whisper, "I do no' ken when, or if ever, I could be a true wife to ye."

There was no doubt to what she was referring. Rodrick had thought about that long and hard before he had proposed to her. "More than anything, I want a wife, a family," he told her honestly. "I want to be a good husband to ye, Muriel. And a good da to yer babe. As fer the rest of it, well, that can wait until ye be ready."

"But what if I am never ready?" she asked.

Then I would have failed in me duty to always make ye feel safe, protected, and important, he said to himself. 'Twas his firm belief that once she was no longer afraid or ashamed of what had happened, she would be able to come to him as his wife. "I would be willin' to wait."

After a long moment, she lifted her gaze and looked him in the eye. "But what if I am *never* ready?"

Rodrick could not resist smiling. "Then I would have lived a good long life, with a wife, a child to call me own, and I would die a happy man." 'Twas nothing short of the truth.

She was deeply touched by his sincerity. The genuineness in his words and tone meant much more than she could ever put to words. It even sent a fluttering sensation through her heart. Muriel studied him closely for a long moment. "If ye be certain of that, then aye, Rodrick, I will marry ye."

CHAPTER SEVEN

With the agreement that they would wait a few weeks to marry— or as long as it took Muriel to grow more comfortable with the idea — they settled into an odd courtship of sorts. 'Twas by no stretch of the imagination a romantic endeavor they were on. Nay, 'twas more of a situation where two like-minded people took the time to get to know one another.

Muriel began to come out of her own shell as well as her hut far more often. During the day, whilst Rodrick trained with Ian and the other men, Muriel would go to the keep to help Rose and Aggie. Most days they worked alongside the other clanswomen, helping to prepare meals for the men who were working daily on the keep or for those who trained. Other days, they worked at sewing and mending or gathering rushes, or tending the gardens.

Now that Muriel was more open-minded about the prospect of keeping her babe, the two women brought their children around her far more frequently.

Little Ada was a beautiful, cherubic babe, with round cheeks, deep blue eyes, and curly red hair. There was no mistaking who her father was, for she had his coloring, but Aggie's beauty. She toddled around the keep, usually in pursuit of her older brother, Ailrig.

Then there was Rose's babe, John. 'Twas difficult to tell yet who he resembled most; his mother or his father. He had blonde hair and big blue eyes. His disposition was such that Muriel believed he was more like his mother than his father, for he was a sweet, content babe. She was certain Ian either did not like her or trust her much, if the scowls and piercing looks were a gauge of such things.

When the weather allowed, the women would take the babes out of doors for fresh air and sunshine. They would not walk far from the protective walls of the keep, at least not without an armed escort. Muriel had known that Rose had been kidnapped not long ago by Rutger Bowie. Rose spoke very little of her time as his prisoner, and Muriel did not want to push the matter by asking too many questions.

The people of the clan were beginning to take notice of her. Most of the women folk were polite and even kind. There were only a small number who looked at her with scorn. Muriel had to assume it was because she was with child and unwed.

While she did find it embarrassing to be in her current predicament, her attitude had begun to improve. When those dark moments reared, she would go to her hut for some quiet reflection. There, she would remind herself that this babe might not be of her own choosing, but it could still be considered a blessing. Silently, she prayed for a girl child with the belief that the risk of it turning out like the man who sired her would be cut dramatically. If she had a boy, Muriel felt she might not end up as lucky as Aggie had with Ailrig.

At night, Rodrick would come for her to escort her to the evening meal. While many of the clans people ate in their own cottages, many invited guests supped with Ian and Rose. On any given night, there were at least thirty people dining in the keep.

After the meal, she and Rodrick would take a long walk together. Some nights they would take several trips around the walls and talk until the midnight hour. Other nights, when the rain was too much, they would sit in Muriel's hut and talk for hours.

Muriel truly began to like Rodrick, not just for the kindness he had shown her, but for his sense of humor as well. There were times he made her laugh until her sides hurt. When she mentioned that to

Rose and Aggie, they thought she was jesting. "I've never thought of Rodrick as humorous," Rose admitted. "Stern, aye, but never humorous."

Her spirits and mood had changed dramatically over the weeks. Muriel no longer prayed for a quick and timely death. Neither did she feel so totally lost and alone. Rose, Aggie, and Rodrick had become more than just friends. They were family.

After her third week amongst the clan, Aggie announced that they would be returning to their own home. They had been gone long enough, according to her husband, Fredrick. Aggie, however, was not as thrilled to be returning as he. "I still do no' feel at home there," she admitted. They were sitting under a tall elm tree as they watched Ailrig and the other children play. John was asleep in Rose's arms, and 'twas all Aggie could do to keep Ada from running after them.

"But it be a grand keep," Rose said. "I would think 'twould be a nice change over where we grew up."

"Did ye no' grow up here?" Muriel asked as she lay on her back looking up at the blue sky poking through the trees.

Rose and Aggie giggled in unison. "Nay," Rose replied. "The original McLaren keep is a mile or two away from here."

"Why did ye move here?" Muriel asked, squinting her eyes against the sunlight.

"Because me father burned the original keep to the ground," Aggie replied bluntly.

They now had Muriel's full attention. She rolled onto her side and looked at them skeptically. "Ye jest."

"Nay, she does no' jest," Rose told her. "'Tis true."

"Why on earth would he do such a thing?" Muriel asked.

"Because he was a mad man," Rose said.

"And because he did no' want me to have it."

Muriel listened as Rose and Aggie told the story of how Mermadak McLaren was not Aggie's blood father. Of how Aggie's mother had been in love with Douglas Carruthers but remained with Mermadak for Aggie's sake. Muriel was dumbfounded to learn that Aggie not only had one keep, but two. Aggie had inherited the

McLaren keep as well as her grandmother Genean Carrruthers' keep a three-day ride north and east of here.

Muriel was about to ask why Aggie did not want to return when Ailrig came up to them. He looked deflated.

"What be the matter?" Aggie asked him as he sat down beside her.

"I want to go fishin'," he said. "But none of the other lads want to go with me."

"Mayhap yer da will take ye later," Aggie told him with an encouraging smile.

"Nay," Ailrig replied. "He be busy with Ian."

Muriel felt truly sorry for the little boy. "Ailrig, would ye take *me* fishin'?" she asked. "Though I must tell ye, it has been many a year since I have done such."

Ailrig raised a brow dubiously. "Ye want to go fishin'?" he asked skeptically.

"Why no'?" she said. 'Twas a gloriously beautiful day, with plenty of sunshine and clear skies. "Unless ye do no' want to go fishin' with a girl?" she said, feigning seriousness.

He thought it a rather odd thing to ask. "I fish with anyone who wants to go," he said. "Man or woman, girl or boy."

Aggie interjected with a protest. "Ye do no' need to take him, Muriel. This boy would fish from sun-up until after sunset if we'd let him."

Muriel got to her feet and stretched her back. "Nay, I do no mind," she said. "I think I would like to impress Rodrick by catching at least a dozen fish."

Ailrig laughed heartily at her declaration. "I wager that would impress him," he said. "I ken fer certain it would impress me."

IN LESS THAN A HALF AN HOUR, AILRIG AND MURIEL WERE SITTING BY the babbling stream with their strings in the water. Rose and Aggie had taken the other children back to the keep, leaving just the two of them alone.

Ailrig was munching on a hunk of bread, propped up on one elbow with his legs outstretched. Muriel was watching the boy out of the corner of her eye. "Why do ye like fishin' so much?" she asked him in a hushed tone.

The boy shrugged his shoulders before answering. "The quiet, I reckon," he replied. "And I like bein' out of doors."

It seemed a good enough answer for Muriel. They sat quietly for a long while, simply enjoying the solitude and stillness.

"It also gives a man time to think," Ailrig said, adding to his earlier response.

Muriel stifled the urge to laugh at him. He seemed so serious and so adult like. "And what would a lad of yer age need to ponder on?" she asked.

He glanced at her out of the corner of his eye. "Ye'd be surprised."

She thought it a rather intriguing answer. "Such as?"

Another shrug of his shoulders was all she received. She was about to ask for further clarification when a fish tugged at his line. With an expertise she thought defied his age, he soon had the fish out of the water, freed from the tiny hook, and placed in the wicker basket. And moments later he had tossed his line back into the water.

Once he was happy with where his line was, he stretched out along the bank, with his hands behind his head and his eyes closed. The more Muriel studied him, the more she began to think he was quite old for such a young boy. Shouldn't he be playing with other children? Mayhap playing with wooden swords and pretending to defend the keep from marauders?

"Mum says ye're goin' to have a babe," Ailrig said quietly.

She felt her stomach tighten for the briefest of moments. "Aye, I am."

"She says ye're goin' to marry Rodrick the Bold."

"Rodrick the Bold?" she asked. "Why do ye call him that?"

"Because that be what everyone calls him," Ailrig replied.

Muriel had to chuckle. "I mean *why* do they call him that?"

Ailrig shrugged his shoulders. "Mayhap because he be a mean son

71

of—" he stopped and corrected his language. "He be a right fierce man on the battlefield, is what I be told. Most people be afraid of him."

"Are ye?" Muriel asked. She wasn't certain how much of this was rumor or truth. She thought back to how Rodrick had helped her escape from the ship. Aye, he'd been more than just fierce. If he hadn't been there to protect *her,* she was certain she might have died from fright alone.

He thought on it for a moment. "Nay, I be no' afraid of him. But neither would I want to anger him on purpose. 'Twould be akin to pokin' a wounded bear with a sharp stick, ye ken."

Aye, she could very well see what he meant. Oddly, she didn't find anything terrifying about Rodrick. Whenever he was with her, he was forever the gentleman. She felt safe with him, safer that she'd ever felt around anyone other than her father. Not even her brother Charles had left her feeling that way.

"I think Rodrick will make a good father," Ailrig said. "Even if the babe be no' his."

A sense of dread and unease fell over Muriel then. She was still filled with doubt about the prospect of marrying Rodrick. And she still clung to the worry of keeping this babe. What if she or he looked too much like Fergus? Would she still be able to love the babe, or would it be naught more than a daily, constant reminder of what had happened?

"I heard mum and da talkin' about it," Ailrig added. "They think I can no' hear them late at night, but I do."

She wondered what else the boy had heard. Suddenly, that all-too-familiar sense of shame came rushing in. She didn't want a boy so young to know that such violent things occurred in this world. And she did not want him to think less of her because of the actions of another. Before she could put to voice what she was thinking, Ailrig was speaking again.

"Can ye keep a secret?" he asked without moving.

Muriel could hear the seriousness in his voice. She remembered having 'secrets' as a little girl. They were naught tremendously important secrets to anyone but herself. They were silly things really, if one compared them to the significance of real, adult secrets or problems.

There was something in the little lad's tone of voice that told her she should not laugh or make light of him, even if she believed his secret 'twas naught more serious than what lass he might 'like' or that he took a sweet cake when his mother wasn't looking. "Aye, I can keep a secret."

Slowly, Ailrig sat up, pulling his knees to his chest. "Ye may no' ken this, but I was bastard born."

Aye, she knew that, for Aggie and Rose had told her. "Aye, I ken that, Ailrig," she replied softly.

He wore the most serious expression. Turning away from her, he stared at the stream. "That used to bother me, when I was younger."

She had to stifle the urge to laugh, for he was still quite young.

"That be no' the secret," he told her. "Me bein' bastard born and all."

With her curiosity piqued, she said, "What is yer secret then?"

"I ken the truth. I ken who me real da is."

IT TOOK EVERY OUNCE OF ENERGY NOT TO GASP OR OTHERWISE LOOK surprised. Muriel didn't know what she should do or say, so she simply listened.

"I heard me mum and da talkin' about it a long time ago. I ken that Eduard Bowie raped me mum."

There was no way to hide her astonishment. She had to look away. *This poor child!* Her heart hurt for him. *What if my own child some day learns the truth? It would be devastatin' for her.* Muriel began to rethink her decision to keep this babe and just *why* Ailrig was sharing this with her. Mayhap she should tell him that mayhap 'twould be best to talk to his parents instead of her.

"At first, it was quite a shock. I was verra angry, ye ken. Angry that no one had told me the truth." He grabbed a blade of grass and began to rub it betwixt his finger and thumb. "But I was even more angry that he had done that to me mum."

An errant tear escaped Muriel's eye and slid down her cheek. *I can no' do that to this babe. I can no' keep a secret such as this, to pretend, to lie. 'Twould no' be fair.* "I am so sorry, Ailrig," she whispered, still unable to look at him.

"Do no' feel sorry fer me," he said. "Because I no longer feel sorry fer meself."

She wiped the tears from her cheeks with her fingertips before looking at him. "I do no' understand." She truly couldn't. How could he not be filled with shame or rage at knowing the truth?

"I ken it might sound odd," he began, "but I ken me mum and da love me. That is all that matters to me. I remember Mermadak, the man who raised mum. He was a mean, cruel son of a whore and I be glad he is dead."

She took note that he didn't correct his foul language and couldn't chastise him for it.

"I be grateful me mum was nothin' like him. I be grateful fer what I have, ye ken. Because, fer a verra long time, me and mum did no' have anything to our names but the clothes on our backs. Fer a verra long time, we lived in constant fear of Mermadak, fear of his beatin's, ye ken."

No, that she did not ken. She knew there was more to Aggie's story than she had shared. Now, Muriel was getting a bigger glimpse at her previous life.

"I also ken I be nothin' like Eduard Bowie, the man who sired me. I will live the whole of me life tryin' to be the opposite of everythin' he was. I will be like Frederick and me mum. I will be a fierce warrior who protects the innocent, just like me da and uncles do. And like Rodrick does."

Now she understood *why* he was telling her these things. He knew the truth about her babe. From his own experience, he was trying to give her *hope.*

Wise beyond his years, Ailrig scooted to sit next to her and wrapped an arm around her shoulder. "Do no' cry, Muriel," he said. "I did no' mean to make ye cry."

Muriel felt absurdly foolish crying her eyes out in front of an eleven-year-old boy.

"I just wanted ye to ken that if ye love yer babe like me mum and Frederick love me, then all will be well," he explained. "All that matters to a child is that they're loved."

––––––––––––––

ALL THAT MATTERS IS THAT THEY'RE LOVED.

Those were wise words from a boy as young as Ailrig.

Muriel wiped away the rest of her tears and took in a deep cleansing breath. "Thank ye, Ailrig," she told him. "I will do me best to remember what ye said."

He patted her shoulder once before scooting away. "And ye'll no' tell anyone that I know the truth?" he asked.

"'Twill be a secret I take to me grave," she told him.

He gave a quick nod before looking back to the fishing lines. After a long moment of silence, he said, "Ye best hurry with catchin' fish, fer I do believe I be winnin'."

Muriel giggled at him. "I did no' realize 'twas a contest."

He looked at her with mouth agape. "Fishin' be always a contest," he said.

Oh, the more she got to know this young lad, the more she liked him. "Verra well then," she said with a smile. "I have nothin' to wager, but let us say that whoever catches the most fish will be declared the King of Fisherman, aye?"

He seemed to like that idea a great deal. "And what shall the loser be declared?" he asked.

"The loser will simply have to live with the shame of losin'."

He nodded in approval. "Do no' worry," he said. "I shall tell no one ye lost."

CHAPTER EIGHT

August arrived and brought more sunshine and heat than Muriel could ever remember in her lifetime. It also brought with it new hope for the future. For days, Muriel thought about what Ailrig had told her that day on the banks of the stream. *All that matters to a child is that they are loved.*

The more time she spent with Rodrick the more she began to believe he would make a good husband and an even better father. If he was willing to look beyond how the babe was conceived, then mayhap she could as well.

'Twas just after the noonin' meal when Rodrick sought her out at the outdoor kitchen. She had just finished washing a pile of pots and pans left over from preparing the noon meal. Her hair was damp from sweating and her dress spotted with water. He didn't seem to mind. "Fancy a walk, lass?" he said as he stood across the table.

With naught better to do, now that her chores were done, she agreed. Wiping her hands off on a drying cloth, she asked Rose for permission. "Go on with ye," Rose said with a smile. "But be back in time to help with the evenin' meal."

Muriel took note of the stern expressions on several of the other women's faces. Thus far, none had been cruel or mean to her. No one taunted her for being an unwed woman with child. Though they weren't treating her poorly, neither were they being as warm and kind as Aggie and Rose. She could only hope that someday they might put aside whatever ill feelings they had for her.

Muriel thanked her and left with Rodrick.

They took their usual route, leaving through the big gate, and walked around the outer wall. "How was trainin' today?" Muriel asked.

"'Twas good," he replied. "The men, I think, are finally understandin' which end of their swords they should use. 'Tis a small victory, but one I will gladly take."

Muriel knew he'd been having an awful time with the men he had been training. There were days he swore 'twas like trying to teach a week-old babe how to use a spoon. "I am glad to hear things are goin' so well," she told him.

Rodrick grunted. "I said they had improved. I didn't say things were goin' well," he told her as they continued to walk around the outer wall. Soon, she heard the sound of the men working on the keep. "Why do ye no' help with the buildin' of the keep?" she asked him.

"I be in charge of trainin' the men," he replied. "As well as in charge of men who guard our borders."

"So ye be Ian's second in command?" she asked.

His lips turned upward, the smile unmistakable. "Aye, I be his second in command."

"That be a verra important thing, aye?" she asked.

"Aye, lass, it is."

She felt proud of and for him. To be the second in command was almost as important as being the chief. Muriel knew Rodrick took his duties very seriously and was glad for it. If he took being a husband and father as seriously as his other duties, then he would indeed make a fine husband and father.

LATER IN THE AFTERNOON, MURIEL FINALLY MET THE HEALER AND midwife of the clan. Angrabraid had to be the oldest person Muriel had ever met. With wrinkled skin, gnarled hands, and a hunch in her back, she looked ancient.

"Ye be with child," Angrabraid said as she stood in the doorway to Muriel's home.

"Aye," Muriel replied, unable to take her eyes off the auld woman.

"I be Angrabraid," the woman said. "Yer midwife."

Muriel stammered for a moment. "'Tis good to meet ye."

"Well, are ye goin' to make an auld woman stand outside all the day long?"

Muriel gave a shake of her head as she allowed the woman in. How could someone *this* auld help deliver a babe?

Angrabraid took a quick glance at her surroundings before slowly lowering herself into a chair. "Do no' be put off by me age," she told Muriel. "Havin' a babe is the most natural thing in the world. Ye will do most of the work. I am just there to see ye do it right."

Muriel suppressed the urge to laugh. "Would ye like a bit of cider?" she asked as she crossed the floor to her small kitchen area.

"Nay," Angrabraid replied. "I can no' stay long. I have other women to see this day."

Muriel put the pitcher of cider back and sat down across from the midwife.

"Do ye ken when ye're due to have this babe?" Angrabraid asked.

While Muriel had a general idea, she was not exactly certain. "I believe in February," she replied.

"A winter babe," Angrabraid said as if she approved of the time of year. "Well, let us see fer certain, aye?"

MURIEL'S SUSPICIONS WERE VERIFIED BY ANGRABRAID. SHE COULD expect her babe to arrive in mid to late February. Silently, she prayed the babe was a girl child.

After Angrabraid left her, Muriel went to the outdoor kitchens to help begin preparing the evening meal. There were a dozen women all working diligently, slicing vegetables, preparing breads and meats, and the other dishes they would serve later that evening.

She looked for Rose and Aggie, but they were not with the other women. Cautiously, she approached the long table, pulled an apron over her head and asked one of the older women, "What would ye like me to do?"

Muriel could not remember the woman's name, but thus far, she had been one of the few who hadn't looked at her with scorn. "Ye can clean these," she said as she placed a big bowl of carrots on the table. "The water be over there," she said with a nod over her shoulder.

Muriel smiled and headed toward the buckets of water. There were two younger women standing near the buckets and they looked at her with nothing less than disdain. Her stomach tightened ever so slightly but she pushed the discomfort aside. *Just show them ye be a good woman,* she told herself. *Let them get to know ye better.*

A FEAST WAS HELD THAT EVENING IN HONOR OF FREDERICK AND AGGIE Mackintosh, for they would be leaving on the morrow. While Rose tried to keep an air of happiness about her, Muriel suspected she was quite sad. Rose's smile didn't quite reach her eyes.

Muriel and Rodrick ate at one of the crowded low tables with a group of warriors. They were not at all a talkative group of men. Mayhap 'twas because she was the only woman at the table and they were silent out of respect. But the rest of the gathering room was filled with lively, talkative sorts. Many people walked by the high table to tell them they would miss Frederick and Aggie.

As soon as Rodrick noticed Muriel was done eating, he rose from the table. "Fancy a walk, lass?"

She could not help but smile at his invitation, even though 'twas the same invitation he had been giving her for weeks. "I would like that," she replied warmly.

Someone at the table grunted, whilst another snorted. There was no mistaking the thinly veiled hostility coming from the men. Muriel felt her face grow hot with embarrassment. Rodrick gave each man a look of warning that turned them mute.

They hadn't taken but a few steps from the table when the formerly mute men began to talk in hushed whispers. Muriel felt Rodrick grow tense as she watched his smile turn to a scowl. His reaction was brief, however, and soon he was leading her through the doors and into the cool night air.

Muriel waited until they were a good distance from the keep before she made mention of what had just taken place. "Your men," she began, choosing her words carefully. "They do no' like me much, do they?"

Rodrick continued to scowl. "Ignore them lass. They be naught but fools."

"Will they ever accept me as one of their own?" she asked.

"It matters no'," he replied. "I accept ye, as does Rose."

But it did matter. She did not want to live the rest of her life as an outcast. "Mayhap, if they knew the truth, that I be no' unmarried and with child by me own choosin', they might think differently of me." The last thing she wanted was to have everyone in the keep know that she had been raped. 'Twas not a discussion she wanted to have with anyone, let alone complete strangers. She was filled with too much shame to do that.

"They will eventually come around, lass," Rodrick told her as they walked through the wide gates. Mayhap 'twas cowardice that kept him from telling her the truth about her brother. Believing it best for now to have her believe the clan's reaction to her was due to her unwed state, he remained mute. Later, after the babe was born, he would tell her the truth.

Muriel knew he was only trying to make her feel better, but it didn't work. While she appreciated the fact that Rodrick, Rose, and Aggie had accepted her, it somehow didn't seem to be enough. She wasn't naive enough to believe the entire clan would want to be her friend, but she needed more than just a handful of people willing to claim such.

For the rest of their walk, Muriel and Rodrick were quiet as each were lost in their own thoughts. After only one trip around the outer walls, Muriel wanted nothing more than to go back to her hut and sleep. 'Twasn't just that she was tired, her heart also felt heavy. She could sense that something weighed on Rodrick's mind, but he was unwilling to share it. "I fear I be verra tired," she told him as they neared the gate.

Rodrick said nothing as he gently guided her through. As they went, Muriel saw three men standing together, passing a flagon of something.

"I do no' care what ye say," one of the men was speaking rather loudly. "Her brother was a traitor."

Muriel felt Rodrick grow tense once again as his back straightened and his face grew dark.

"But that does no' mean *she* be a traitor," another man said as he took the flagon and drank from it.

"I say we give the lass a chance."

Muriel came to an abrupt stop and listened. In her heart, she knew they were talking about her.

"Come, Muriel," Rodrick whispered as he tried to pull her along.

"Charles McFarland was a traitorous bastard," the third man said. "I will wager ye, his sister be one as well."

Stunned, Muriel looked into Rodrick's eyes. "They lie," she managed to murmur.

From the pained expression in Rodrick's eyes, she knew the truth at once.

―――――――

RODRICK FELT AS THOUGH HE HAD BEEN KICKED IN THE GUT. "MURIEL," he stammered. "Let me explain."

Her eyes were filled with horror as she took a step back. "Nay," she exclaimed. "They lie!"

He took her by her elbow and began to lead her toward her hut. "I will explain it to ye," he told her. "But let us go to yer hut first."

She yanked her arm from his grasp. "Tell me now," she said angrily. Standing her ground, she crossed her arms over her chest and waited.

Rodrick raked a hand through his hair as he tried staring her down. "'Tis a conversation best had alone."

"Why do those men think me brother a traitor?" she demanded.

Rodrick thought back to Ian's words of warning. *Ye best tell her before someone else does.* Oh, how he regretted his decision now, to keep the painful truth from Muriel. "Yer brother *was* a traitor," he was trying to be calm and rational, but 'twas not easy, considering the look of murderous rage she was giving him.

"Ye lie!" she cried. "How could ye rescue me if me brother was a traitor?" she asked. "Why did ye no' just leave me to rot?"

He wasn't about to tell her about the haunting dreams he had suffered from weeks ago. Dreams that disappeared the same day he rescued her from Skye. "Because 'twas the right thing to do," he told her.

"The right—" she paused and shook her head. "I do no' believe ye. No' any of ye!" She spun around and ran toward her hut. Rodrick was right behind her.

MURIEL RAN AS FAST AS HER LEGS WOULD TAKE HER, BUT RODRICK WAS faster. Before she could slam the door in his face, he was rushing over the threshold. "Ye must calm yerself down and listen!" he shouted.

Muriel scurried away and stood with her back pressed against the wall. "I will no' calm down!" she yelled back.

"Aye, ye will," he told her as he stood just inches away. "Charles did betray this clan. Every last member."

Before she could scratch out his eyes, he grabbed her wrists and held them tightly. "But he did it fer *ye!*"

Stunned, she looked up at him, awash in confusion and hurt. "What?"

Rodrick took in a deep breath and let it out slowly. "Instead of comin' to me, his friend, he sided with the Bowie chief. He did it fer ye, to try and earn enough coin to get ye released from Kathryn McCabe-MacDonald."

Her brow furrowed into a knot of confusion. "I do no' understand."

"'Twas all a plot to take over the Mackintosh and McLaren clan. It was a plan a long while in the makin'."

Muriel shook her head in disbelief. "Why would Charles do such a thing?" she asked, unable to find a clear answer.

Rodrick didn't understand it either. "He did what he thought was best in order to get ye back."

Tears streamed down her cheeks as she looked at him for any signs at all that he was not speaking the truth. But there were none.

How could Charles have done such a thing? "Why did ye no' tell me this sooner?" she asked.

He expelled a quick breath of frustration. "I did no' want to cause ye any more pain."

How could she find fault in that? From the first time she had met him, he had done nothing but try to protect her, to keep her safe. But this? This secret? "Ye should have told me," she said. "Now I understand the people here do no' care that I be unwed and with child. They are upset because they think me brother a traitor."

"I be sorry, Muriel. I should have told ye sooner."

She studied him closely for a long moment. "I do no' fault ye fer yer decision," she told him truthfully. "I be tired now. I think ye should leave."

Although she was not angry with him, she was angry at this new turn of events. Thankfully, he did not argue with her. He bid her good night before quitting the hut.

MURIEL DID NOT SLEEP WELL AT ALL THAT NIGHT. HER MIND WAS KEPT far too busy with the disturbing news about her brother. Charles had betrayed this clan. He had done it for her.

Angrily, she tossed and turned most of the night. How could he have done such a thing? Why did he not go to Rodrick, who was supposedly his friend, and ask for his help? She supposed she would never have the answer to that burning question. She could live to be one hundred years old and never have an answer.

But what of Rodrick and her plans to marry him?

Everything the man did was motivated by his strong sense of honor. Of doing *the right thing* or protecting those in need.

Aye, those were fine qualities. What woman wouldn't want a man such as he?

But what of the rest of the clan? Would they ever be able to trust her? Would they ever be able to look at her without thinking of Charles? Could she live the rest of her life amongst the people her brother had betrayed?

It didn't matter to them *why* he had betrayed them. The fact still was and would always remain the same: he had done the one *unforgivable* thing.

And what of this child growing in her belly? What kind of life would she have, labeled the niece of a traitor? This babe's future was already bleak at best. Add Charles's actions to the mix and Muriel could see no hope at all for her future.

Before dawn, Muriel came to a decision. A decision that would most certainly hurt Rodrick. But for the first time in weeks, she finally made a decision *for* her child.

She needed to leave this clan.

CHAPTER NINE

Muriel's only hope at a decent future lay in the hands of Aggie and Frederick Mackintosh. With a heavy heart, she went to them before the sun began to crest on the horizon and pleaded for their help. Frederick left the final decision up to his wife.

"Are ye certain?" Aggie asked as they stood on the steps of the keep. "What about Rodrick?"

In her heart, she believed Rodrick deserved a far better wife than she could ever be to him. It hurt to admit such, but Muriel felt 'twas best for all of them. "Ours is no' a love match," she said. "This be his home. I can no' ask him to give up the life he has made for himself here."

It did not take long for Aggie to make her decision. "Verra well," she said. "Ye may come with us."

Why it hurt to hear Aggie agree, she was uncertain. Mayhap she had grown accustomed to the idea of living *here*, with Rodrick as her husband. But she *was* thinking of him, of his future just as much as she was thinking of her babe.

After a brief discussion on how she would actually get to the

Carruthers' holding, it was decided that Muriel would ride with one of Frederick's men. She did not wish to ask Ian for a mount, feeling they had already done more for her than she deserved.

Muriel hid and watched from the rear of the procession, as Aggie and Rose, Ian and Frederick, said goodbye to one another. She felt every bit a skulking coward for leaving like this, but she did not want to give either Rose or Rodrick the chance to talk her out of leaving.

This, she believed, was the right decision for everyone concerned.

'TWAS NEARING MIDNIGHT BY THE TIME MURIEL AND THE REST OF THE band of Mackintoshes rode through the gates of the Carruthers keep. Her bottom was sore and her bones ached, but not nearly as much as her heart.

For the entire sojourn North, she kept telling herself this was all for the best. Rodrick was better off without her. At least here, her babe stood a better chance at a brighter future. Still, she felt a tremendous loss and deep sorrow at leaving Rodrick.

'Twas difficult to see the keep and all its glory at this late hour. Muriel could only suppose it was a beautiful place and quite grand if the silhouette against the backdrop of the moon was any indication. Opulence or hovel, it mattered not to her. This was to be her last new beginning.

They took a narrow set of stairs up and into the keep. Through a short and narrow portico of sorts, they were immediately met with three sets of stairs. One to her left, one to her right, and one straight ahead. She found it rather odd until Aggie explained it had been built more for defense than anything else.

Quite generously, Aggie and Frederick gave her one of the smaller rooms on the third floor. 'Twas nicely if sparsely appointed. One small bed in the far corner, a table and two chairs were placed under a narrow window. A brazier burned low in the center of the room. A large trunk rested near the door. Beside it was a small table holding a basin and pitcher and a few washing cloths. Other than that, there was naught much to the space. She reckoned it truly didn't matter.

"On the morrow, we shall set ye to work in the kitchens," Aggie said from her spot near the doorway. "Then we can discuss what lies ahead fer ye."

"I can no' thank ye enough, Aggie," Muriel said with a weak smile.

Aggie embraced her warmly. "'Twill be good to have a friend here," she replied.

Muriel thought it odd she should say such a thing, but she was too tired to inquire as to why she'd said it.

After Aggie left, Muriel slipped out of her gown and into the warm bed. After not sleeping much the night before, she was asleep almost at once.

RODRICK WAS FURIOUS.

Muriel had left before dawn, with Aggie and Frederick Mackintosh. She didn't even say goodbye. She just *left*. Without explanation or warning.

Rose had waited until noontime to tell him. Her excuse was that she sincerely felt Muriel needed time to digest what she had learned about her brother. "She is hurtin'," Rose told him. "Mayhap she just needs a bit of time to sort things out in her head."

Rodrick glowered at her.

"Think on it, Rodrick. She has had much happen to her in such a short amount of time. She be afraid, and now embarrassed over what Charles did."

His expression turned darker, yet he remained silent. His head was spinning with worry, frustration, and aye, anger.

"Mayhap after a few days, she will come to her senses."

Rodrick raised a brow and shook his head in disgust.

Rose studied him closely for a long moment before her eyes grew wide as if she had just discovered something. "Ye love her!"

With his lips pursed together, he crossed his arms over his chest. "Please fergive me, m'lady, but that be none of yer concern." 'Twas a fact he'd come to realize only recently. As yet, he was not willing to admit it to anyone, let alone Rose.

Rose took a step back, her lips turning upward with a good measure of satisfaction. "Ye men be all the same," she declared. "Ye can fall in love with a woman, but ye'd rather rot than admit it to anyone, least of all yerselves."

Aye, she had the right of it, but he would not agree openly with her assessment. For Rodrick, this was a deeply personal matter.

"Let Ian ken I will be leavin'," he told her as he turned to leave the gathering room.

"Shall I tell him where ye be goin'?" Rose asked, her tone laced with sarcasm.

"To get me future wife," he shot over his shoulder.

I'll no' be comin' back without her.

MURIEL SLEPT LATE, THOROUGHLY EXHAUSTED FROM THE EVENTS OF THE past two days. Even though she had not eaten much the day before, it all still came up, leaving her feeling quite lightheaded and tired. But she knew she could not lay abed all the day long.

Guiltily, she rushed to dress when she realized she had probably already missed the morning meal. *What will Aggie think of me?* She cursed under her breath. "It be a fine way to start yer first day here," she muttered as she slipped her feet into her slippers. "They will think ye naught but a lay-about."

She splashed cold water on her face, ran her fingers through her hair and hurried out of the room.

Last night, before she fell asleep, she had promised herself she would awake feeling much better about being here. She would also set aside any guilt she felt at leaving Rodrick the way she had.

"It be a new day," she said as she descended the stairs. No matter how hard she tried to put a smile on her face and hope in her tone, it didn't work. She still felt miserable.

When she came to the second floor, she was met by a rather hard looking woman of mayhap fifty years of age. Silver hair braided around her scalp framed a face that mayhap at one time could be considered pretty. Her stern expression, however, did little to make Muriel feel at home.

"Sleep the day away where ye come from?" the woman asked.

Taken aback, Muriel tried to apologize, but the woman would have none of it.

"Ye may be one of the new mistress's friends, lassie, but ye'll still be expected to work. I will no' be trottin' up and down the stairs waitin' on ye hand and foot, no I will no'."

Muriel didn't know if she should feel angry or afraid. She went with the former. "Excuse me," she said, doing her best to affect a stern tone of her own. "But who *are* ye?"

"Ye may call me Mrs. MacFaddon," she said with a scowl. "Now, off below stairs with ye. The new mistress says ye are to be workin' in the kitchens. The day be half gone now as it is."

Without so much as a *good day, lass,* the woman hurried down the hallway.

A sense of dread fell over Muriel's shoulders. Silently, she prayed the rest of the people here were not as hard as Mrs. MacFaddon.

Muriel rushed down the steps and landed in the small portico. 'Twas as dark and forbidding a place during the day as it was at night. If her memory served correctly, the center door would lead her to the gathering room. Hopefully, there would still be someone about who could direct her to either Aggie or the kitchens.

The door was heavy and groaned loudly when she pulled it open.

The first thing she thought when she stepped inside was, *Poor Aggie!* The place was dark and dreary, nothing at all like Aggie, who was always bright and cheerful.

The second thing she thought, when she caught sight of the lone figure who turned around to face her was *run!*

Rodrick was standing in front of the cold hearth.

And he did not look at all happy.

Nay, not one bit happy.

What she could make of his expression in the dim light — all dark and furious looking — set her fingers to trembling.

Before she could turn around and run, the door behind her closed with a soft thud. Suddenly, she found she was unable to speak. Mayhap that was best, considering the look of murderous rage staring back at her.

A heartbeat later, he was thundering towards her. He did not stop until her back was pressed against the heavy wooden door.

Blood rushed in her ears as her heart beat heavily against her breast. She wasn't afraid of him, at least not afraid in the sense that he was going to bring her any physical harm. But she was afraid nonetheless.

Without permission or warning, he bent low and kissed her full on the lips.

'Twasn't at all the kind of kiss Fergus had slobbered her with.

Nay, 'twas a soft and gentle kiss that said a thousand different and terrifying things all at once. Not terrifying as in impending doom or fear of attack, but terrifying in how it made her feel. 'Twas a gentle, sweet kiss filled with warmth, adoration, and a few things best left unspoken, at least for now. It surprised her that she was not appalled by it, or sickened, or horrified.

A moment later, Rodrick took one small step back. "Gather yer things," he said, still glowering and looking more than just a bit perturbed. "We be leavin' at once."

His words returned her to her good senses. Pulling her shoulders back, she said rather defiantly, "Nay," she gulped once. "I do no' believe I will."

Rodrick's scowled darkened. His words were clipped and his tone stern. "Yes. Ye. Will."

"Let me explain to ye *why* I left," she began, her tone curt and direct in an attempt to match his.

"I ken exactly why ye left," he told her. "Ye worry people will look at ye with scorn and malice for what yer brother did."

A bit surprised, she said, "Aye, that is part of it."

"Ye also believe I deserve better than ye."

Silently, she cursed Aggie or Frederick for betraying her confidence. Somehow, one of them had told either Rose or Rodrick the *why* of her leaving. "Then ye can understand why I can no' come back with ye."

"Nay, I do no'." He said, still looking angry.

Muriel rolled her eyes in dismay. "I do no' ken how much clearer I can be. I can no' live amongst people who will think me a traitor because of me brother's actions."

"They will only think ye a traitor or coward if ye leave like this," he said. "If ye come back with me, ye will be showin' them ye are neither of those things."

While he did in fact make perfectly good sense, she was not sure she was up to the task.

"And *I* want ye to come back," he told her.

She knew there was more he wanted to say, but coward that she was, she did not feel brave enough yet to hear it.

"If ye do no' agree to come back with me, then I shall stay here until ye change yer mind." The hard angles of his jaw were set. His brown eyes were filled with a determination that was unmistakable. No wonder he was considered such a fierce warrior.

An unfamiliar sensation, akin to a flutter of butterflies, grew in her chest. "I can no' ask ye to give up everythin' ye have worked so hard to build." She knew he had searched for years to find a place where he felt at home.

"Then come back with me."

Never in her life had she met someone as determined as Rodrick. His countenance left no question that he would in fact remain here, giving up everything he had worked so hard for.

Muriel growled, let out a frustrated breath, and threw her hands up in the air in defeat. "Verra well," she told him. "But I return under protest."

Looking victorious, he smiled and raised a brow. "And what is it exactly that ye be protestin'?"

"I do no' think the clan will ever accept me," she told him.

Rodrick shrugged his shoulders with indifference. "The better question is, will *ye* accept *them*?"

CHAPTER TEN

After saying goodbye and thank you to Frederick and Aggie, Rodrick and Muriel left the Carruthers' holding. With Muriel perched in front of him, Rodrick steered *Caderyn* back to the Mackintosh and McLaren keep. He knew she was furious and frustrated, but he did not care at the moment. He had won. Somehow, he had managed to convince her to go with him.

They had ridden more than an hour in stony silence before Muriel finally spoke to him again. "I want to know the entire truth about how me brother died." 'Twasn't a question, 'twas a full out order. Rodrick chose his words as carefully as a healer chooses her herbs. One wrong statement and Muriel might very well climb from the horse and run back to the Carruthers' keep.

"I was no' there when he died," he told her honestly.

"Where were ye?" she asked, apparently forgetting what he had told her weeks ago.

"I had been injured," he reminded her politely. "I was recoverin'." He hoped she wouldn't ask *how*.

She turned slightly to look up at him. "How were ye injured?"

God's teeth, he did not want to tell her the truth. "That be no' important."

"I think it is," she said, scrutinizing him closely.

Looking straight ahead, he focused on the horizon. If he lied, she would know it or eventually find out the truth. "Charles tried to kill me."

Her eyes widened in horror as her mouth fell open. For a brief moment she might have thought he was jesting. Then she saw the seriousness of the matter etched on his face. "Why on earth would he do such a thing?" she asked in bewilderment. "I thought ye were friends?"

"I thought so as well. Until he stuck the dirk in me chest."

Unable to continue looking at him, Muriel turned away. After a lengthy silence, she said. "I be so sorry, Rodrick."

He could hear the tears in her voice. "Do no' fash yerself. Yer brother did what he thought he must do to protect ye."

It had taken a few months of trying to figure out Charles's actions before Rodrick finally understood. A desperate man will sometimes do things that do not make a lick of sense. While he might never forgive Charles for trying to kill him, Rodrick at least understood his motivation. Everything he did was for Muriel.

"Why did ye come fer me?" she asked in a low, hushed tone. "And please, do no' tell me 'twas the right thing to do."

Rodrick fell silent while he debated on whether or not he should tell her about the dreams.

"Rodrick, I would like to ken the why of it. It has to be more than a simple sense of honor. Me brother tried to kill ye, yet ye fought to rescue me. Fer the life of me, I can no' understand why."

The *why* of it might take a lifetime to explain. However, if he were ever to expect her to be honest with him, he would need to be honest with her. "I began to have dreams," he said. "Verra vivid dreams in which a bonny lass was crying out to me fer help. I assumed that lass was ye."

Turning again to face him, her face bore an expression of sheer perplexity. "Ye came to help me because of a dream?"

"Aye," he said. "I did. 'Twas a dream that plagued me fer weeks."

"Plagued ye?" she asked.

"Aye," he said with a nod. "It haunted me, Muriel. 'Twas the same each time. Ye were asking me to help ye."

"But how did ye know who I was? How did ye know who to look for? We had never met," she said with a bit of disbelief and wonder.

He smiled warmly. "As yer brother lay dyin', he told Ian about ye. Later, I found letters from Kathryn McCabe written to Charles. Whilst a description of ye was never given, I knew ye were in dire need of help."

"And ye rode all the way to Skye to find me," she said. "All because of a dream."

He could see it did not make much sense to her how a once complete stranger would or could come to someone's aid like that. Hell, he still wasn't sure he understood it himself. "'Twas more than just a dream," he said. "In me gut, I knew ye needed help. I could no' just ignore the dreams, or ye."

Dumbfounded, she could only stare at him incredulously. Everything he had done, every act, every risk taken, was all because of a dream. She supposed she should be grateful to him for listening to it, for if he hadn't? She shuddered to think of where she would be right now if he had ignored the ethereal pleas for help.

Had she not begged God for His help? Had she not cried for months, pleading with Him to send Charles to her?

And that day, when she was being forced aboard Captain Wallace's ship. Had she not then begged for someone, *anyone* to help her?

Studying Rodrick closely for a time, a sense of calm began to drape over her heart. God *had* answered her prayers in the form of a hardened warrior named Rodrick the Bold.

With her head held high, Muriel returned to the Mackintosh and McLaren keep with Rodrick. Borrowing some of his courage — for he seemed to possess a never-ending supply of it — she woke the following morning with a new sense of determination. If whatever dark deed her brother had done did not matter to Rodrick — who had very nearly died by Charles's own hand — then it should not matter to anyone else.

While she did receive a few curious looks and even fewer hard stares from the clanspeople, no one had much to say. At least not to her face. If anything, she was met with cool silence.

Muriel dived into her daily routine with determination. While she would not bring up the subject of her brother, she was fully prepared to respond should anyone else be so inclined. She would agree that he had in fact behaved most deplorably as it pertained to the clan. She would even go so far to admit that he his actions had been traitorous. However, she would also politely explain the reasons behind his actions. If they still could not forgive Charles, so be it. But she refused to allow anyone to hold her responsible for his actions. Nay, everything lay at the feet of Rutger Bowie, for 'twas he who had started the entire sordid affair.

After the first week since returning, she was growing more and more frustrated. No one, not one single person had anything to say on the matter of Charles. What was the use of having a properly laid out retort if one couldn't use it?

Later that night, while she and Rodrick walked around the outer wall, he sensed her upset.

"Ye be awfully quiet," Rodrick noted.

Pursing her lips together, she let out a rapid, frustrated breath. "Did ye tell everyone no' to discuss the matter of me brother with me?"

"Nay," he replied, his brow drawn into a curious wrinkle.

Muriel chewed on the inside of her cheek for a time. "I fear I do no' understand it then. No one has said anything to me about him since our return." While they might not have said anything, she had the oddest sensation that at least a handful of them wanted to give her a piece of their minds.

Rodrick shrugged his shoulders. "I remember somethin' one of the men who raised me used to say. *Do no' go borrowin' trouble.*"

"I do no' think I am borrowin' trouble," she told him curtly. "I am simply wonderin'—"

"Why it is no' one is burnin' ye at the stake?" he asked with a grin. "Lass, I tell ye that ye need to stop worryin' over things. The people will either come around or they will no'. All ye can do is show them who *ye* are."

"And who am I?" she blurted out, uncertain anymore she could answer that question.

Rodrick stopped and smiled warmly. "Ye be a good, bonny lass who is goin' to marry this scraggly, old, scarred warrior someday."

"Ye be no' old," she argued.

Rodrick chuckled at her reply. "But I still be a scraggly, scarred warrior, aye?"

"I would no' call ye scraggly either." While she could not begin to call him handsome, she wasn't quite sure what she would call him. But scraggly? Nay, he was not that.

"What would ye call me?" he asked playfully.

Uncertain if he were only teasing or being truthful, she answered as honestly as she was able. "I would call ye a good, kind man," she replied, her cheeks growing warm with just a bit of embarrassment.

Her answer seemed to please Rodrick, for he laughed and chuckled off and on for the next hour or so.

She could live to be a thousand years old and would never understand men.

CHAPTER ELEVEN

Fergus MacDonald had nearly forgotten about the pretty lass whom he had once derived great pleasure from. Though he had been quite displeased to learn someone had helped her escape from Seamus Wallace's ship, it was of no importance to him. The lass was gone from his life now and he didn't give a rat's arse what happened to her. At least not in the beginning.

Anthara refused to procure another pretty young woman to work in their home. He loved his wife, he truly did. And not just for the large dowry and small fortune she had brought into their marriage, although that did help.

Nay, he loved her because of her undying devotion to him. No matter what he said or did to her, or anyone else for that matter, she would either look the other way or defend him with an unyielding and betimes terrifying allegiance.

They had been married for five years and had yet to be blessed with a child. More than anything, Anthara wanted a babe of her very own. But thus far, God hadn't seen fit to allow Fergus's seed to plant itself within her womb.

Truth be told, Fergus didn't really care one way or the other. Or at least he hadn't until his older brother Gerome came to visit him. Their father had changed the terms of his will again.

Fergus now sat in his private study, drinking the finest whisky, and staring at the low-burning embers in his hearth. Reflecting once again on what Gerome had told him earlier that day, in this very room.

"Da will cut ye off by the end of the year," Gerome had informed him, *"if ye do no' produce an heir."*

"Why does it matter if I have an heir or no'? I am the lowly third born son," Fergus had asked as he watched his brother closely.

Feigning ignorance, Gerome shrugged his shoulders. "Who kens what makes our father do what he does?"

Fergus was quite certain his dear brother Gerome was to blame for their father's sudden decision.

"All I ken is that we must all produce heirs or we will no' inherit anything," Gerome said.

"Considerin' ye already have three children of yer own, and Traigh has two, and Willem has five, none of ye have anythin' to worry over, do ye?" Fergus kept his fury hidden behind a mask of indifference.

Gerome let loose with a heavy breath, doing his best to look concerned for Fergus. "I am only here to tell ye what father has asked me to."

Fergus did not believe for one moment that Gerome was the all-concerned oldest brother. "So I must produce an heir within the year or our lovin' father will cut me out of the will," he said for the sake of clarification.

"No' only will he cut ye out of the will, he will stop givin' ye yer monthly allowance."

Fergus took another long drink of the amber liquid and continued to fume. He and Anthara could live well enough on her dowry alone. 'Twasn't as if their survival depended on the paltry monthly allowance. Still, it grated on his nerves, the audacity of his father's new edict. Produce an heir or be cut off completely. 'Twas as great an injustice as ever done to him, Fergus believed. 'Twas bad enough he was the third born, and worse still that too many people to count were already ahead of him in line of succession. Most of the MacDonald clan would have to be wiped out by a famine or a disease, or the keep burning to the ground with them in it before Fergus stood a chance at ever becoming their chief.

The sound of Anthara's voice broke through his quiet reverie. "Are ye comin' to bed soon?" she asked from the doorway.

As yet, he had not told her of his father's edict. Wanting to put off what he was certain would be a tear-filled, panic-stricken event with his wife, he nodded. "I shall be right up."

For the first time in his life he found himself praying that his seed would take root. However, he fully doubted those prayers would be answered.

CHAPTER TWELVE

After weeks of courtship, where not a kiss — save for the one at Aggie's keep — or flowery word had been exchanged betwixt them, Rodrick and Muriel were married on a bright, crisp winter's day, just a week before the Christmas Tide celebrations were to begin.

Muriel was beyond nervous. Her fingers trembled in tune with the heart beating ferociously against her breast. While she tried to convince herself that 'twas naught more than what any woman would feel on her wedding day, her heart begged to differ. He was more than a friend; he was her protector, and soon, he would be her husband.

But love him? Nay, she could not say 'twas love she felt for him. At least, not in the romantic sense. She truly and sincerely *liked* Rodrick. He was a good, honorable man. Not only would he make a good husband to her, he would be a wonderful father to her child.

There was no naivety on her part, as it pertained to how he felt about her. Without question, she knew he had fallen in love with her. Though he hadn't given her the words to confirm it, the way he looked at her said everything. There was always a glint of adoration and fondness in his bright eyes whenever he glanced her way.

That twinkle went well with the warm smiles or grins. While most of the womenfolk thought him a hard-looking man, Muriel thought him quite handsome, in a rugged sort of way.

The ceremony took place in front of the hearth in the Mackintosh and McLaren Keep. Evergreens and holly hung overhead as a great fire burned in the hearth. Every clan member was in attendance to witness Rodrick the Bold marry the lass from Edinburgh that bright day.

Rodrick and Muriel each promised to honor and cherish one another, to always be honest and kind, and to take each day as a gift.

Rodrick promised to protect her unto his dying breath if needed.

Muriel promised to be a good wife to him in any way she was able.

Rodrick made a silent promise to one day bring Fergus MacDonald's head to Muriel.

Muriel made a silent promise to try to love this kind, honorable man, and to at least keep an open mind about someday being a *true* wife to him.

Even if she never came to him that way, Rodrick knew he would have everything his warrior's heart ever wanted. Everything he had wished for since he was a lad: a wife, a bairn, and a home of his very own.

ONCE THE PRIEST ANNOUNCED THEY WERE GOODLY WED, HE GAVE Rodrick permission to kiss his bride. He and Muriel had discussed the wedding kiss beforehand, simply because he did not want to do anything that would cause her any amount of upset. Muriel had decided that one little kiss would not hurt, for 'twas Rodrick kissing her, not Fergus MacDonald. He had also made a most heartfelt promise that after the wedding kiss, he'd not kiss her again without her permission. 'Twas a promise she was grateful for, she supposed.

Rodrick looked into her eyes and quirked one brow as if to ask her once again if a kiss was acceptable. Muriel nodded once before taking in a deep, fortifying breath. He had kissed her before, back at Aggie's keep. While she had in fact liked that kiss, it had terrified her all the same.

His lips curved into a warm smile right before he bent his head to press his lips against hers. With his hand on the small of her back, he did not pull her against his chest, as if to claim her as his like some violent, hard man might.

'Twas just as sweet as the last time he'd done it. She did not feel sick to her stomach, nor was she overcome with horrification or disgust when his lips touched hers, nor did she have the urge to scream and run away.

'Twas not a passionate kiss, but 'twas just as romantic as one. There were many unspoken promises hidden in it that did not pertain to passion or desire. Nay, his kiss – so warm, soft, and sweet – was a promise that said he would always keep her safe, would always make her feel protected and adored.

Muriel needed to feel that sense of safety more than she realized.

RODRICK DID HIS BEST TO MAKE THE KISS AS CHASTE AS POSSIBLE. WHILE he desperately wanted Muriel in the physical sense, he kept his urges and desires in check out of respect. He hoped that, with time and patience, she would eventually come around to the idea of a physical relationship with him. Her worry, he knew, was that she might not ever be able to do that. If she couldn't, that fault would lie with him, not her. He was determined to do everything he could to make her feel safe and protected, for he believed that was the key.

The kiss did not last nearly as long as he would have liked. It took all his strength to pull away. When he did, he saw something in Muriel's eyes that made him feel near giddy with joy; she understood his message. *I'll never harm ye. I will always keep ye safe.*

Muriel smiled up at him with such fondness it made his toes tingle with glee. The smiled reached her pretty eyes, making them sparkle. Relief settled in over his shoulders; she was not afraid.

Happy with that small step in the right direction, he placed her hand in the crook of his arm and turned to face the crowd. Rose looked at the two of them with happy, damp eyes. Ian was smiling as if he had finally come around to the idea that Muriel was not the traitor her brother had been.

The men cheered and whistled, while the women folk gave nods of approval. Hopefully, their approval would continue on for many years.

WITH THE CEREMONY OVER, A SMALL AFTERNOON LUNCHEON WAS HELD in the keep in honor of the newlyweds. 'Twas not a grand feast, complete with musicians and dancing, or vast amounts of ale and wine. Just a small gathering with a handful of warriors, Ian and Rose.

The air in the keep was calm and peaceful, yet still happy. They supped on meats, cheeses, breads, and fruits whilst talking in small groups in hushed tones.

Ian stood at the head table and cleared his throat, drawing everyone's attention. Raising his cup, he looked at Rodrick and Muriel, who sat at the end of the table. "To Rodrick the Bold and Muriel. May ye have many years of peace and happiness together."

The crowd cheered in agreement and drank to the newly married couple. Ian did not take his seat, for he was not done speaking.

"I must admit, I never thought Rodrick the marryin' kind," he winked at Muriel. "I never thought there would be anyone brave enough to agree to it."

The crowd laughed in agreement. No one had thought Rodrick the marrying kind.

"To Muriel," Ian said as he raised his glass to her. "The only lass in all of Scotia brave enough to marry Rodrick the Bold!"

Rose giggled and added, "Mayhap we should call her Muriel the Brave?"

The guests cheered and drank. Muriel's face flamed red. Under her breath she said, "I certainly do no' feel brave."

Rodrick patted her hand. "But ye are lass," he said with a warm smile. "Fer ye have married me."

WITH THE SPECIAL MEAL OVER, RODRICK AND MURIEL WALKED ARM IN arm to the small hut. The little hut that would now be *their* home together. Pausing at the door, he pushed it open. With a wide, beaming smile, he scooped Muriel up in his arms.

She squealed, more out of surprise than anything else.

"What are ye doin'?" she asked him incredulously.

"Carryin' ye over the threshold, lass," he smiled down at her. "'Tis customary, or so I be told."

Without another word, he carried her inside, kicking the door shut behind him.

Were the circumstances different, he might have tossed her on the bed. Instead, he carefully set her on her feet and looked around the space. A new, bigger bed had been brought in by persons unknown. Rodrick had a sneaking suspicion the bed was due to Rose.

Dried flowers had been hung over each window and a vase of them sat in the center of the table. A fire had been lit, along with numerous candles. It smelled to him of home and warmth.

"Lass, I dare tell ye, it has been many a year since I have slept in a home of any kind," he admitted.

Muriel had not moved from the spot where he'd placed her. Nervously, she worked the edges of her cloak with her fingers.

"Me family died when I was young, ye ken," he went on to tell her. "I was all of nine."

Tilting her head to one side, she studied him closely for a moment. In the past weeks, he'd only spoken of his childhood in general and vague terms. Curious, she asked, "Who took care of ye?"

"Warriors," he replied softly. He did not like to speak of those times, of his youth, of losing his family. It always made his heart feel empty. "I have told ye that before, have I no'?"

She gave a slow shake of her head. "Nay. Ye told me ye lost yer family to the ague, but no' much else."

With a shrug of his shoulders, he pulled out a chair and offered it to her. Muriel, feeling a bit more comfortable, began to remove her cloak. It took him only two steps to reach her. With a smile, he helped her out of her cloak and into her seat. He sensed her anxiety but said nothing of it. After hanging the cloak on the peg by the door, he took the chair opposite her. Stretching out his long legs, he rested an arm on the table. "There be no' much to tell," he said. "I lost me family to the ague."

From her expression, she was not convinced there was naught more to his life than that. "And what happened between then and now?" She asked with a quirked brow.

Talking seemed to put her at ease. While he was never comfortable sharing most of his life's story with anyone, he decided it would be best if he put his pride aside for at least a little while. "The ague destroyed our small clan," he began. "There were less than fifty of us when 'twas over. Mostly men."

"All warriors?" she asked as she absentmindedly rubbed her belly.

"Mostly warriors," he replied. "There was a handful of younger men and even younger lasses. I was the youngest."

"How did ye all survive then?"

He offered her another shrug of indifference. "'Twas no' easy," he said. "But we somehow managed to make it work."

Pursing her lips together, she studied him closely for a moment. "'Tis no' easy fer ye to talk about it, is it?"

"Nay, lass, 'tis no'."

Drumming her fingers on the table, she chose her next words carefully. "'Tis no' easy fer me to talk about what Fergus did to me."

Lifting a brow, his face turned hard. He did not want to think about Fergus MacDonald, especially not on this special day. "Lass," he began before she cut him off.

"Ye ken my time with them was the darkest, ugliest time of me life. If ye want me to trust ye, then I would hope ye would trust me."

He hated to admit it, but she was right. Expelling a heavy sigh, he nodded in agreement. "I was raised by hardened warriors. Men who taught me how to fight, how to protect the keep. They taught me how to wield a sword, to fight with me bare hands. They taught me many things, lass…"

"But?" she asked, urging him to continue.

"They taught me how to survive, to fight, to hunt, and what it means to be a warrior. They did no', however, teach me how to speak from me heart. In fact, such things were frowned upon." Growing uncomfortable, he began to slowly spin the vase of flowers.

Muriel smiled warmly. "But methinks ye learned anyway."

Uncertain what she meant, he asked for clarification.

"Rodrick, there be many ways of speakin' from the heart. 'Tis no' just words a man says, but his actions that tell just as much, sometimes more, than words."

Looking up from the vase and into her eyes, he felt his face grow warm with just a bit of embarrassment. A grown man, he was blushing like an innocent lass who'd just learned how babes were made. Her beautiful eyes were filled with understanding.

These two lonely people had somehow managed to find one another amidst the chaos and cruelty that life or fate — or whatever one chose to call it — oft threw into the paths of unsuspecting individuals. They were now embarking on one of life's grandest adventures: marriage. However, 'twas not what one might consider typical or even average. Nothing about these two people could be considered typical or average.

They sat in quiet contemplation for a long moment. The fire crackled, the flames of the candles dancing in the invisible breeze wafting in from the tiny windows.

Rodrick knew not what he should say or do. 'Twas late in the day, but not so late as to climb into bed.

"Tell me more," Muriel said, finally breaking the silence. "What kind of child were ye?"

Before or after the ague took me family? There was quite a distinct difference between the two. Letting out a heavy breath, he began to toy with the vase again. "Before me family died, I reckon I was like most lads of that age," he began. "Busy playin' with me friends, helpin' me family with our little farm, pretending to protect kith and kin against invaders and dragons." He chuckled softly at old memories of his childhood, of the time before it all fell apart. "If ye were to ask me da, I was a precocious boy, oft into trouble of one sort or another. But if ye were to ask me mum, I was naught but an angel."

Muriel smiled warmly at him, showing straight white teeth, her eyes twinkling in the candlelight. "Ye? An angel?" she asked playfully.

"Aye," he replied, returning her smile. "Were me mum still alive, she would tell ye as much."

"Methinks yer parents would have been verra proud of how well ye grew up," Muriel said with much sincerity.

Rodrick could only hope she was right.

THEY SAT, THIS NEWLY-WEDDED PAIR, FOR SEVERAL HOURS, SHARING their happiest memories from their childhoods. The conversation helped to set both of them at ease, to take their minds off the fact this was their wedding night.

Several times, Muriel got to her feet to walk around the small space, to stretch her back, for it was growing more uncomfortable for her to sit for long lengths of time. There was no denying the fact she was with child, for her belly was round. Though she was in her seventh month, Rodrick still thought her the most beautiful woman he had ever had the pleasure of knowing.

'Twas nearing the midnight hour when Muriel began to yawn, rubbing her lower back with her palm. Rodrick stood, stretched his own arms out wide, and said, "I think it be time fer us to lay our heads down."

The smile left her then, as her eyes darted from him to the bed and back again, fearfully. He could not resist the urge to smile. "Lass, ye can have the bed," he told her. "I shall sleep on the floor."

Inwardly, she wrestled with her fears for a long moment. *I have to put me fears aside and trust this man,* she told herself. "Nay," she finally said. She could not expect the poor man to sleep on the floor for the rest of their lives. To expect as much was unfair to both of them. Besides, he had given her his promise, on multiple occasions, that naught would happen until she agreed to it. "We can sleep in the same bed, Rodrick."

Raising a brow, he asked, "Are ye certain?"

"Aye," she said with a smile.

'Twas difficult, to say the least, for Rodrick to climb into bed with her each night and resist the strong urge to take her in his arms. Refraining from touching her or kissing her took Herculean strength.

But refrain he did.

They slept side by side each night, each doing their best not to touch the other. It went on like that for weeks, with Muriel sleeping on the outside edge of the bed, clinging to its side. However, as time went on, it became more and more difficult for her to sleep in such an uncomfortable position.

Late one night, as she was in a deep sleep, she rolled over, grunting ever so slightly as she brought her burgeoning belly with her. Before he knew what was happening, she was snuggling into him, as best she could, and tossing an arm over his chest.

Rodrick held his breath. Uncertain if he should gently move her arm away or mayhap give her a gentle nudge, he remained as quiet and as still as a snow-covered loch. Closing his eyes, he breathed in her scent. 'Twas a blend of flowers and warm bread that lingered from their evening meal. Intoxicating and maddening all at once.

Deciding he should allow her to sleep, he pretended for a long while that she loved him as much as he loved her. Pretended that she wanted him in the physical sense, that no harm had ever been done to her. 'Twas reckless – he knew it – but he could not help himself.

Ye'll burn in hell someday, he whispered to himself. *Ye risk hurtin' her heart more than yer own.*

He'd rather be gutted and have his entrails dipped in oil and set afire than to hurt her. But for just a little while, he would allow himself to dream.

They had been married less than a sennight when Rodrick presented Muriel with his gift and promise. Muriel was getting up to clear the table when he stopped her. "Please, lass, sit for a moment."

Reluctantly, and with a look of concern etched across her brow, she retook her chair. She was still quite cautious when it came to him. Especially if he was within arms' reach. He hoped his gift would help put her caution and ill ease to rest.

"There be somethin' I want to give ye," he said. Leaving her at the table, he went to his cloak and removed the small bundle that was wrapped in soft linen. Smiling, he sat back down and placed the bundle in her hands.

"What be this?" she asked.

"Open it," he said with a nod toward it.

Carefully, she placed it on the table. She untied the bit of leather and pulled back the linen. Confused, she looked up at him.

"'Tis a *sgian dubh*, lass. Yer verra own," he explained with a good deal of pride.

Tears welled in her eyes. His chest felt constricted, for he thought he'd done something wrong. "I meant for it to make ye smile, lass, no' cry!" he explained. "To make ye feel safe."

She remained quiet as she studied it without touching it.

Wanting very much for her not to cry, Rodrick continued to explain the meaning behind the gift. Taking it in his own hands, he showed her the intricately carved handle. "See? This be a wolf," he told her as if she couldn't see it. "Those be little garnets in his eyes, ye see. And wrapped around him is the MacElroy plaid. 'Tis the MacElroy banner, ye see."

The tears she'd been fighting gallantly to hold onto began to slip down her cheeks. So quiet was she that he was growing more and more concerned. "Lass, I did no' mean to make ye cry."

Muriel wiped away the tears with her fingertips and took in a deep breath. "I ken that. These be happy tears, Rodrick."

He could live to be a thousand years old and never understand why a woman cried when she was happy. Letting out a quick sigh, he scratched the back of his head in confusion.

"Ye give me this because ye want me to feel safe, aye?" she asked as she took the *sgian dubh* from his hand.

"Aye," he replied in a low voice. "I want ye to always feel safe."

Finally, she smiled. "Thank ye, Rodrick."

"Ye're most welcome, lass," he said. "But there be more."

She raised a brow and asked him what he meant.

"After ye have the babe, I want to teach ye how to defend yerself. Not only how to use the *sgian dubh* properly, but how to truly defend yerself."

All manner of feelings tumbled around in her belly. Predominately and at the forefront was a deep sense of gratitude.

"Would ye like that?" he asked.

Nodding her head, she said, "Aye, I would."

Feeling better, he smiled and patted her shoulder with one hand. "Good. We shall begin in the spring, after the babe is born and ye have fully recovered."

She too was feeling much better, as well as a bit playful. "I want ye to teach me everythin'," she said.

Rodrick chuckled. "Well, I do no' ken if ye want to ken *everythin'* lass."

Quirking a brow, she said, "But I do."

He stared at her in quiet disbelief.

"I even want to ken how to best *ye*, should the need arise."

His laugh all but shook the little hut. Deep and booming it was. "Och! Lass! If ye ever do learn to best me, ye'll be the first person on God's earth to do so."

MURIEL'S BELLY CONTINUED TO GROW AS THE DAYS WENT ON. RODRICK did not seem to mind it at all. Each morn he would wake with a cheerful smile and ask, "How is me beautiful bride this morn?"

She thought it rather silly that he would think of her that way. She certainly didn't feel beautiful. But she did feel better. Better than she had expected to or even believed was possible just a few months ago.

He was just as patient as he had promised he would be. But then, they'd only been married less than a fortnight. 'Twas a quiet worry that rarely left her thoughts that mayhap, someday soon, he would have enough of their *marriage in name only* and either demand she perform her wifely duties or, worse yet, leave her.

Still, he was so kind to her. On the second day after they were wed, he had built a dressing screen with his own hands. He told her 'twas so she might have privacy when changing and not have to worry about him seeing her in a state of undress by accident. She had a sneaking suspicion he did not want to keep going out into the cold air whilst she changed.

On the fourth day, he hung curtains in the far corner of their hut. Curtains that hid their chamber pot. Again, so that she could have privacy.

Muriel asked naught from him. She didn't have to. 'Twas as if he could read her mind. He brought water in from the well each morn, as well as wood he used to set the fire. When he saw she was tired or uncomfortable, he would wrap a fur around her shoulders whilst rubbing her shoulders.

Thrice a week he would fill a tub with hot water so that she could have a good, long soak.

He had procured sweet smelling soaps and soft cloths for bathing. He had even purchased fabric with which she could make clothes for their babe.

Each gesture was genuine. Rodrick was not doing these things to impress her. These sweet gestures came from the purest of places: his heart.

Her fondness for him grew with each passing day. In return for his kindness, she cooked for him, mended and washed his clothing, and kept their hut as neat and tidy as possible. Anything she could think of, she did, to show him she was grateful. Anything, save for the physical intimacy shared between most husbands and wives.

RODRICK AND MURIEL SOON FOUND THEMSELVES FALLING INTO A comfortable routine. Each morn she would prepare his breakfast, then he would head off to train the men. They had to be trained in shifts because so many of them still needed to work on the construction of the keep. Rodrick would stop long enough to race back to their home to eat, then race off again. Depending on the weather — and at this time of year the weather often dictated with supreme indifference — he might be gone from dawn to dusk.

On one particularly sunny afternoon, just after the new year, Muriel decided to take Rodrick's lunch to him, instead of waiting for him at home. 'Twas a bright, clear day, with only the hint of a breeze. The earth and everything around them was blanketed in snow. But the men had made paths from the cottages to the kitchen tents and to the keep, to make the trek easier for one and all.

With booted feet, she trudged through the snow with a basket of food draped over one arm. 'Twas not as easy as she had anticipated, what with her big, cumbersome belly. Still, 'twas nice to be out of doors and breathing in the fresh air and soaking up the sun.

Muriel heard the men before she saw them. Metal clashing against metal rent the air. She heard much grunting and cursing as she rounded the corner of the keep.

There, on the wide-open yard, were two-dozen men. Not a one of them wore their winter fur cloaks. A few of them were even bare-chested!

One of those bare chests belonged to her husband.

He was in the center of the yard, wearing only his black leather trews and fur-covered boots. His long dark hair was pulled back at the nape of his neck, tied in place with a bit of leather. Sweat covered his wide chest and well-muscled, taut arms. The sun glistened off him, casting him in a near ethereal glow.

In one hand was his sword, in the other, a dirk, as he fought with a man a good ten years younger than himself, and at least a head taller.

The sight of Rodrick, his muscles wound tight, his jaw set firm, stole her breath away.

Instantly, a wave of guilt washed over her. After all she had been through, after everything Fergus had done to her, here she was, enjoying the sight of her half naked husband. The guilt was all consuming. She should not be feeling this way toward any man, or so she believed. Did wanting to reach out and touch his bare chest, to feel his lips pressed against hers make her naught more than the whore Fergus had told her she was?

Tears filled her eyes as her stomach roiled with self-reproach. Turning away, she all but fled the safety the shadow of the keep offered.

LIKE A COWARD, MURIEL SKULKED BACK TO HER HUT. ONCE THERE, SHE placed Rodrick's meal on the table and began pacing. What she wanted more than anything was to speak to Aggie Mackintosh, but she was an entire day's ride away. Rose, being Aggie's dearest and closest friend, would have to do. Hopefully, she would be able to answer the questions scattering about Muriel's mind and heart. Wrapping her cloak around her, she set off for Rose's home.

Rose smiled when she saw Muriel standing at her door. "Muriel!" she said with a smile as she opened the door to allow her in. Rose offered her a seat at the table while she went to peek on her son. He was sleeping contentedly in a cradle by the fire.

"What brings ye here this day?" Rose asked after handing Muriel a mug of warm cider.

Muriel was uncertain how she should broach the subject.

Sensing her unease, Rose placed a warm hand on top of hers. "What is it?" she asked in a soft voice. When Muriel did not immediately answer, she asked, "Be it Rodrick?"

The tears fell then, softly and slowly trailing down her cheeks.

"What has he done?" Rose asked. "Do I need to gather the women folk and hang him?"

Muriel laughed, albeit only slightly. She appreciated Rose's sense of humor. "Nay, Rose. He has done nothin' wrong."

"Then why did you cry at the mention of his name?" she asked.

Letting out a heavy breath, Muriel fought to find the right words. "This would be so much easier talkin' to Aggie about."

"I thank ye fer the compliment," Rose said, feigning insult.

Muriel laughed half-heartedly again and swiped away her tears. "I meant no insult to ye," she said. "It just that Aggie *understands*."

Realizing immediately what Muriel meant, Rose nodded her head. "Tell me what the problem be," Rose said. "And if I can no' help ye solve it, then we shall send fer Aggie."

Muriel shrugged her shoulders, awash in embarrassment and uncertainty. "Well," she began. "I went to take Rodrick his noonin' meal." Oh, this was far more difficult to discuss than she had imagined.

"And?" Rose said after much time had passed.

"Well, he was trainin' with the men, ye ken." Her throat suddenly felt quite dry, so she took a sip of the cider.

Rose began to drum her fingers on the table. "Muriel, ye can talk to me about anythin', ye ken that, aye?"

"He was wearin' naught but his trews and boots," Muriel whispered ashamedly.

Rose remained silent for brief time as she reasoned out why *that* would cause her friend such upset. When understanding settled in, she smiled. "I take it 'twas a site to behold?"

Muriel could feel her face burn with humiliation and shame. Unable to keep it all in, she let the tears and words flow. "I be naught more than the whore Fergus accused me of bein'!" she blurted out.

"Of course not!" Rose scolded her.

Muriel shook her head in disagreement. Choking on her tears and frustration she said, "Aye, I am! After everything he did to me? To be thinkin' me husband a fine-lookin' man? To want him to kiss me? Nay, that makes me everything Fergus said I was and worse!"

Rose knelt before Muriel and took her hands in her own. "Nay, Muriel, that be no' true."

Shaking her head, Muriel said, "Ye do no' understand."

Smiling affectionately, Rose said, "I may no' have gone through what ye have, Muriel. But I have talked to Aggie many a time about it. Do ye think *she* believes she be a lowly sort of woman fer desirin' Frederick?"

"Nay," Muriel replied reluctantly. "But 'tis different fer them."

"Why?" Rose asked, raising a pretty brow.

Muriel shrugged, for she wasn't quite certain herself. "They love each other," she murmured.

"Think ye that Rodrick does no' love ye?"

"But —" Muriel began.

Rose cut her off with a heavy sigh. "Lass, he does love ye. Anyone with two eyes can see it. And me thinks ye might have some feelin's of warm regard for him, aye?"

"Of course I have feelin's of warm regard for him," Muriel admitted. "But that does no' mean that I should be havin' *those* kinds of feelin's!"

Rose giggled softly. "'Tis only natural," she replied. "But think about this for a moment," she said as she returned to her seat. "Ye *are* havin' those good feelin's towards yer husband."

'Twas clear to Rose that Muriel did not clearly understand her meaning.

"That be a good thing," Rose said. "It means Fergus's hold on ye is growin' weaker and weaker. It means Rodrick's love for ye and kindness to ye is allowin' ye to move on. To move away from those black, dark times in yer life."

It took a long moment before Muriel began to clearly understand what Rose meant. When clarity set in, she let her breath out in a rush and her shoulders finally relaxed. "I had no' thought of it that way," she admitted, wiping her damp cheeks with her fingertips.

Rose continued to smile warmly at her. "Ye might no' be ready to be his wife in every sense of the word," Rose added, "but at least ye be headin' in the right direction, lookin' forward instead of behind ye."

"I be glad I came to see ye," Muriel told her.

"That be what friends are for," Rose replied. "I will always be here for ye, Muriel."

Today was filled with many firsts for Muriel. 'Twas the first time she felt any kind of physical attraction toward her husband. 'Twas also the first time she felt like a normal young woman. And for the first time in a very long while, she believed she truly did have a good friend.

CHAPTER THIRTEEN

'T was long after the midnight hour when Muriel woke Rodrick with three little words that can evoke fear in even the bravest of men. Words that have made the legs of many a man since the dawn of time weak and tremble. Words that can cause a man with a sound mind to babble like an idiot.

"Me waters broke," she whispered harshly.

Like an arrow shot from a crossbow, Rodrick leapt from the bed. Standing in naught but his braes — the undergarment he wore only out of respect for his wife — his eyes were wide with horror. "Now?" he stammered in horror. "But I do no' ken how to help ye!"

Muriel rolled her eyes at him. "Ye daft man," she began as she rolled herself out of the soft bed. "'Tis no' like she will be born in the next moment."

"Oh," he replied, the horror fading from his face, but still coursing through his veins.

As he stood like a lummox, watching his wife struggle to her feet, he felt seven kinds a fool with his feet apparently frozen to the floor. His mind went blank as his heart hammered against his chest.

'Twasn't until she was on her feet that he was able to move. "What should I do?" he asked, afraid to touch her or move any closer.

"Go get Angrabraid," she told him.

"Right," he replied with a quick nod. Spinning on the balls of his feet, he tore open the door with such force Muriel thought he'd unhinged it.

"Rodrick," she called to him softly.

He stopped and spun to look at her.

"Ye might want to at least grab a cloak," she said. "It be a might cold outside."

Shaking his head, he looked at her with astonishment. "I be a warrior, lass. 'Tis a short walk to Angrabraid's."

Muriel raised a brow. "Aye, 'tis true. But ye might want to cover yerself nonetheless."

When he noticed she was staring at his chest, then his lower regions, he took a gander at himself.

Slapping his hand to his forehead, he went to dress as quickly as possible.

JUST AS THE SUN WAS BEGINNING TO RISE THE FOLLOWING MORN, Muriel pushed her wee baby girl into the world. Rose bundled the bairn into swaddling cloth as Angrabraid stepped outside to give the news to Rodrick and Ian.

Rodrick, covered from head to toe in fur, looked like a giant bear about to pounce on an unsuspecting animal. He was pacing back and forth, running his hand through his hair, looking every bit the worried husband and father. Angrabraid clucked her tongue and shook her head. *Men!* She mused. *They'd rather fight a horde of rabid wolves disemboweling a cow than be anywhere near their woman when it came time to birthin'.*

"'Tis a fine lass," she told Rodrick as she drew her shawl around her hunched shoulders. "A wee, bonny lass."

Rodrick stopped his pacing and stared at her with wide, fear-filled eyes. He was not quite ready yet to set aside his worry. "And Muriel?" he asked, holding his breath.

"She be fine," Angrabraid told him. "A strong woman, yer wife is. A good, strong woman."

The breath left him in a loud whoosh as his shoulders sagged with relief. Ian slapped him on the back and smiled. "A lass," he said, feigning sadness. "Ye have me sympathies."

"Sympathies?" Rodrick asked incredulously. "Why be ye givin' me yer sympathies? Did ye no' hear Angrabraid?" He didn't bother with waiting for Ian's reply before rushing into the cottage to be with Muriel.

THE MOMENT HE WALKED INTO THE TINY HUT AND LOOKED AT HIS WIFE, he nearly fell to his knees. Though her hair stuck to her head from hours of sweat and birthing pains and dark circles had formed under her eyes, Rodrick thought she looked so magnificently beautiful it bordered on the celestial.

'Twas the look of utter joy and happiness painted on her face that nearly did him in. In her arms she held their tiny babe, bundled in swaddling cloth. And Muriel was smiling and speaking to her in hushed, motherly whispers.

For weeks he had worried she would change her mind and want nothing to do with their babe, that she would turn the child away, and in turn, him. In his heart, he knew he couldn't have blamed her or held her in low regard if that had been her choice. Aye, it would have devastated him, but he would have understood.

Muriel slowly tore her affectionate gaze away from her daughter and looked up at him. "Rodrick," she smiled up at him with damp eyes. "I would like ye to meet yer daughter. "

All at once, every worry he had ever held onto, every fear, fell away. The tension, the doubts were now gone. Expelling a quick breath, he rushed to Muriel and knelt beside her, using every ounce of courage to fight back his own tears.

For a long while, he could not tear his gaze away from his wife, such was his relief and utter joy. This moment would forever be burned into his memory and his heart.

"She be a bonny wee lass, aye?" Muriel asked as she looked fondly upon the bundle in her arms.

Finally, he looked down at the babe.

Then back again at his wife.

And back to the babe who sported an entire head of dark red hair.

He'd never met Fergus MacDonald, but he was quite certain this child resembled him in every way.

Red hair.

Muriel's hair was a beautiful shade of golden blonde. His own was dark brown.

There would be no way they could pass this innocent babe off as his.

For the entire time he had been pacing out of doors, he had only one concern: the safety and wellbeing of his wife and child. Not once had it entered his mind that this babe would resemble the man he now desperately wanted to see burning in hell.

Words were lodged in his throat, and for a long, long moment his heart did not beat. Muriel's previous worries about the child reminding her of Fergus had come true. This babe, innocent as she was, would forever be a constant reminder of the son of a whore who had raped Muriel and nearly destroyed her.

He began to worry that he could not love his babe as his own.

"Would ye like to hold her?" Muriel asked as she began to hand the babe to him.

Sucking in a fortifying breath, he shook his head ever so slightly. "I've never held a bairn—"

Muriel did not allow him to finish his protest as she placed the babe in his shaking arms.

All he could do was stare down at the babe in dumbfounded incredulity. One little hand was balled into a fist, the other wrapping itself atop her wee head. Atop her *red-hair* covered head.

"Look at ye!" Muriel exclaimed, albeit weakly. She sounded tired, worn out, and done in, but proud all the same. "I do believe she likes ye."

Lord, how he wanted to feel a sense of overwhelming pride! Of fatherly devotion, of some form of kindness, but for the life of him, those feelings would not come.

Red. Hair.

He could not get past the red hair and the fact that no one would ever believe the child his.

Muriel was speaking to him, but he did not, could not hear her. His mind was a swirl of doubt, dread, and anger. Nay, he was not angry with the innocent babe sleeping most contentedly in his arms. He was angry, nay furious, with the man who had sired her. The man who had hurt his sweet Muriel to the point she had at one time wished and prayed for her own death. The man who had hurt her to the point she could not stand the thought of being a wife to him.

Fury towards a man he'd never met. A man who had somehow managed to steal away Rodrick's dreams and hopes for a happy future with wife and bairns.

There was only one thing to be done about it. He was going to kill Fergus MacDonald if it was the last thing he ever did on God's earth.

***

MURIEL SENSED RODRICK'S UNEASE, BUT SHE BELIEVED 'TWAS SIMPLY born of the fact he'd never held a newly born babe before. He was staring at their babe — and yes, that was how she chose to look at this child, as theirs — with such a look of fright, that she almost giggled. Here was her strong, braw husband, so tall and manly, and he was done in and turned mute by a tiny babe.

Muriel stretched, wanting very much to sleep for a good long while, but her heart was filled with so much happiness, she knew 'twould be next to impossible. This overwhelming sensation of love and adoration toward her child was beyond her reasoning. She had not expected to feel this way about her.

Doubt and worry had been her constant companions these many

months. But the moment Angrabraid placed the babe on her belly whilst she cut off the cord, all those feelings flew away in the blink of an eye. And when she heard her daughter cry for the first time? All she could do was weep with joy and relief.

"I dare say I never thought to feel this way about her," she admitted to Rodrick. "But from the moment I saw her, I knew."

Rodrick's gaze seemed to be glued to their daughter and he remained awfully quiet.

"And when I saw all that red hair?" she said with a smile. "Och! I must admit I was verra glad to see it."

Rodrick, upon finally hearing her, lifted his head so quickly she was surprised his neck didn't snap. "What?" He asked, sounding perplexed if not a bit horrified.

Muriel smiled fondly at her husband. "I said I was verra glad to see all that red hair."

"But why?" he asked, his eyes wide with puzzlement.

"Me da had red hair," she told him. "He would have been so proud to have a grandchild who looked like him. Charles and I, we have our mum's colorin', ye ken."

There was no mistaking her husband's relief. His breath came out in a great whoosh as his shoulders sagged. She understood then, why he'd remained so quiet. "Ye worried the red hair was a gift from the man who sired her," she said, unable to be angry with him for she too, had worried over that very thing.

Rodrick was fighting hard to find the right words to deny her accusation. Guilt and worry filled is green eyes.

With a slow shake of her head, she smiled up at him. "Rodrick, do no' fash yerself over it. Each of us had the same worry, aye?"

SUDDENLY, HE FELT SEVEN KINDS OF A FOOL FOR WORRYING OVER something so insignificant as the color of his daughter's hair. But he could not deny the relief he felt when he learned his wee daughter took her grandsire's coloring.

Looking back at the babe, he smiled for the first time since seeing her only moments ago. "She be a bonny lass, aye?" He all but beamed with pride and adoration.

Rose piped up from across the room, where she had been busy sorting through bloody sheets and cloths. "I should think so!" she declared. "She looks just like her mum."

Rodrick had to agree. She *did* — sans the red hair — very much resemble her mother.

"Have ye named her yet?" Rodrick asked as he touched the babe's cheek with his index finger.

"Aye, I believe I have," Muriel replied sleepily. "I would like to call her Cora."

Rodrick's eyes grew damp as his heart constricted with nothing short of unadulterated love toward his wife. "After me mum?" he managed to stammer out.

"Aye, after yer mum," Muriel said.

God's teeth! He mused silently. *But these women are fully intent on seein' me cry this day!*

CHAPTER FOURTEEN

Was there not an old adage that said *Good things come to those who wait?* Fergus was certain he had heard that saying before, but for the life of him he could not remember when or where. He supposed it didn't matter at the moment, for the information he had just overheard was far more important.

While 'twas a frigid spring day, with gray, gloomy skies out of doors, the tavern was warm. Warmed more so by the pretty wenches who served him his food and drink. Silently, he had hoped none here would recognize him or ask for his name. He was sitting in a dark corner of the tavern in the fishing village of *Camhanaich*.

Fergus had come here in hopes of finding a new housemaid. One that he could use and one that his wife would find no objections to. Due to the reputation he'd garnered on Skye, most young women refused to work in his home. Deciding it best to leave the island in search of a suitable young woman, he had stopped here to eat and rest a bit before resuming his search.

But now? After eavesdropping on the conversation at the table next to his, he felt more than just warm. He was downright giddy as he reran it over and over in his head.

"I never thought I would see the day that Rodrick the Bold would dote after a lass nor a babe," the older of the two men had said. *"But see it I have, with me own eyes."*

"Ye jest," came the reply of the younger man with long blonde hair and a scar running across his forehead. *"It can no' be the same Rodrick the Bold I ken from his days with Clan MacElroy."*

"I tell ye it is!" The old man argued before taking a long pull of his ale. *"He walks around showin' the bairn off to anyone and everyone."*

The younger man whistled and shook his head in disbelief. *"She must be a fine woman, to make Rodrick hang up his sword."*

The older man laughed heartily. *"She must be, fer the babe be no' even his!"*

"What?" The younger man asked as he leaned in closer. *"How can that be?'*

The older man shrugged his shoulders. *"I do no' ken who the babe belongs to, but it be no' Rodrick's. He came back last year, havin' rescued the lass from some ship captain. Stole her right off the Isle of Skye, he did."*

That had been when Fergus's ears perked up like a wolf hearing the scurrying feet of an unsuspecting rabbit. *Ship captain?*

"Aye," the older man nodded when the young man whistled again. *"Captain Wallace, I believe his name was. I was told,"* he said, leaning across the table to share his secret, *"that the captain bought the lass off Fergus MacDonald. Right angry, Wallace was, fer he had no' had the time to enjoy her as he wanted."*

"Did Wallace go after them?"

The old man gave a nod and a wink. *"Fer a few days. But he had to turn back, fer they could no' delay any longer."*

Fergus downed his mug of ale and did his best not to smile. His gut told him Muriel's babe was *his*.

Oh, how his father and brother were going to eat their pride!

His father's edict said nothing about the *legitimacy* of an heir. Not one word. His mind raced with images of his father's crestfallen face when Fergus would present his new grandchild to him. *"I have sired a babe,"* he would tell him. He would, of course, feign a great amount of fatherly pride toward the bastard babe. But he had to wonder if his wife would accept his cast off as her own? *Of course she would,* he mused. Anthara wanted a babe of her very own, more than she wanted anything else.

This babe would be all the proof they needed that their lack of children was her own fault, not his. She would have to accept the cold hard truth of it. And when she did, she would be so busy tending to her new child, so filled with joy that she would look the other way while he had his fun.

He tossed a few pieces of silver on the table and quit the tavern. He had to return to Skye and gather a few hardened men who would not balk at taking a babe from its screaming mother's arms. As he all but skipped back to the ferry, it suddenly dawned on him that he did not know if the child was a boy or a girl. It did not matter. All that mattered was that he had in fact sired a child.

Och! Me da and brothers will rue the day.

CHAPTER FIFTEEN

Rodrick stood in the gathering room, looking into the worried eyes of his laird. They had just finished listening to two young men who patrolled their borders give them most disconcerting news.

"Ye be certain 'twas Randalls that attacked?" Ian asked.

"Aye," said the one name Thomas. He was a tall, gangly man, with long light brown hair and blue eyes still filled with astonishment and fear. "Ten of them," he added.

Ian's jaw was clenched, his eyes filled with fury. The Randalls had just raided their southeastern border. Thankfully, no one was killed, but one of his men was seriously injured. The reivers had made off with five head of cattle to boot.

They could ill afford any losses at the moment, whether it be men or precious livestock. For more than a year now, they had been busy rebuilding all that Mermadak McLaren, their former laird who was now burning in the bowels of hell, had torn asunder. It would be years before they could breathe with any amount of relief. Years of hard work lay ahead before the clan would ever get back to the fine, large a clan it once was.

This raid could not have come at a worse time.

Ian looked at Rodrick. "I say we visit the Randalls," Ian said. "And get our bloody cattle back."

Rodrick nodded in agreement. He looked just as mad as Ian. "We need to make certain the keep is guarded well," he said. "The Randalls might be usin' this as a means to attack while we are away."

Ian nodded, his lips pursed, his brow drawn into a hard line. "The bloody bastards!" He ground out.

Rodrick grunted. "They be more mercenary than anything," Rodrick offered. "There be somethin' off about all this."

"We have never had issue with the Randalls before," Ian said. "I never thought them allies, but I never felt the need to worry over them."

"Ye worry over *everyone*," Rodrick said. "Unless they be yer blood kin, ye should trust no one."

Ian turned his attention back to the two young men. "Go, get a meal and a wee dram to settle yer nerves."

The two men cast wary glances at one another before Thomas asked, "What then?"

Ian glanced first to Rodrick before answering. "Then prepare yerselves fer battle."

RODRICK HATED TO LEAVE HIS WIFE AND DAUGHTER FOR ANY LENGTH OF time. He most especially did not wish to leave them alone after the Randall raid. Who knew what the sons of whores were up to. The raid could have been a means to inspire an angry retaliation that would leave the keep and its people weak and unguarded. But neither Rodrick nor Ian were foolish enough to make such a mistake.

Muriel could not hold back her tears. "I ken it be selfish," she told him. "But I do no' want ye to leave us."

He kissed the top of her head as he pulled her to his chest. "Wheest now, lass," he whispered. "I shall be back on the morrow."

Truth be told, he was glad she would miss him. Aye, 'twas undoubtedly a selfish thing to think and feel. But it had taken them months, nearly a year, to get to this point in their relationship. No longer did she balk at hugging him, or telling him what was in her heart. She had yet to give him the words he so desperately wanted to hear, and as yet, they had not consummated their marriage.

"Ye promise?" she asked him.

"Aye, I do so promise."

RANDALL MEN WERE EASILY BOUGHT. THERE WAS VERY LITTLE THEY would not do for a bit of coin. Little still for even larger amounts. With the Bowie clan having laid down their weapons and thieving ways and now busy with farming, it left a gaping hole of sorts in Scotia. The Randalls were all too eager to help fill the gap left behind by the Bowies' departure from lives of crime.

Leon Randall, the chief of Clan Randall, was as desperate a man as any. After years of failing crops, of raids upon their lands, there were more cobwebs in their coffers than coin. Therefore, when he was visited by one Fergus MacDonald and his promise of coin in exchange for a few nefarious bad deeds, he could not say no. He had too many mouths to feed. Too many people counting on him to get them through yet another miserable winter.

Therefore, in the spring of 1358, he set his plan in motion. They would raid the Mackintosh and McLaren clan in hopes of drawing out enough of their men to set the second part of his plan in motion.

If everything went well — and he could only pray that it would — in a week's time, he would have enough coin in his coffers to see his people through the next two years. That was all he wanted; to keep his people from starving.

Aye, desperate times often call for desperate measures.

BEFORE DAWN THE NEXT MORNING — AFTER TEARFUL GOODBYES WITH their wives — Ian Mackintosh and Rodrick the Bold led a small contingency of men out of the gates of the Mackintosh and McLaren keep. Rodrick was not even out of the gates when the deep ache of missing him settled over Muriel's shoulders. She stood for the longest time, watching them ride away until the men were naught but specks on the horizon. 'Twas not until she returned to their home that she let the tears fall. And fall they did, like spring waters over the *Mealt falls*.

These feelings of longing and worry caught her completely off guard. Muriel hadn't expected to miss her husband as much as she did. But 'twas undeniable. She missed him to the point of a deep, physical ache.

A question — which was at first, quite horrifying — loomed before her as large as the *Aonach Beag* mountain. Had she fallen in love with her husband?

As she sat near the brazier, with Cora sleeping contentedly in her arms, Muriel allowed herself the chance to think on it. Would it be such a bad thing to love her husband? He was a good, kind, decent man. A man who had been nothing but good to her for the better part of a year. Rodrick had the patience of Job when it came to Muriel. Not once in all these many months had he ever made a demand of her. Not even a simple request had fallen from his lips as it pertained to anything physical betwixt them. Nay, he hadn't pushed, nor insisted nor begged.

Suddenly, the question of whether or not she loved her husband did not seem so horrifying. Nay, it left her with such a sense of calm and peace that it stunned her.

Muriel began to think of her conversations with Aggie Mackintosh, those many months ago. *"I had given ten years of me life to the man who raped me,"* she had told her. *"I realized one day that I did not wish to give him another moment."*

Were it that simple? To simply free oneself from the past? To once and for all set aside the fear, the shame and guilt and move on with your life?

Looking down at her sleeping babe, Muriel began to weep again. Cora. This tiny, innocent, beautiful babe had been born out of an act so deplorable, so ugly and harsh that it hurt to remember it. How could something this innocent have come from such an ugly deed? It didn't seem possible or even logical, but 'twas true all the same. Cora was precious, sweet, and innocent. She represented hope for the future.

Aye, it still stung, still hurt to think of all those times Fergus had hurt her. It still made her stomach churn with disgust at the memories of those awful moments. But oddly enough, Muriel didn't feel quite as guilty or ashamed now. Nay, she had not asked for any of those things to happen to her. She had not been a willing partner; she had been a victim. A victim of fate, circumstance, and Fergus MacDonald.

Months ago, she had prayed for her own death, in order to escape the shame and horror. Back then, she wanted nothing more than to lie down and die, so that she could finally forget. But now? Now, she was a mother and a wife. Mother to a babe she had never believed she could love as much as she did. And wife to a most remarkable man. A man, she was now certain, she loved.

Rose and Aggie had been correct when they assured her that everything would change after she gave birth to her child. Muriel smiled warmly and shook her head slightly. 'Twas a pleasant surprise to realize they had been right.

MURIEL DID HER BEST TO KEEP HERSELF BUSY IN HOPES IT WOULD MAKE the day go by faster. With wee Cora strapped to her chest in a sling, Muriel busied herself in her gardens for most of the morn. Pulling out offending weeds and watering those plants that needed it took up very little of her time.

She spent the rest of the day tending to her babe and cleaning their little home, which was already immaculate by most people's standards. That eve, she dined in the keep with Rose and Deidre Mackintosh and their wee ones. Of the five men who left that morn, only three were married. While Rose and Deidre did their best to present themselves as happy, Rose knew they were missing their husbands just as much as she.

"I imagine they will be back by the evenin' meal on the morrow," Rose declared while she fed bits of beef and vegetables to her son. He was an adorable babe, not quite a year old yet.

Deidre agreed with a nod and a smile. "Sooner if I ken our husbands."

Muriel knew that Rodrick could take care of himself, as well as the men who rode with him. Still, she worried. What if they came upon dozens of Randalls? How could five men defend themselves against such a number?

Hearing her babe whimper pulled Muriel from her quiet reverie. She put Cora to her breast and smiled.

"She be a beautiful babe," Rose told her with a warm smile.

Deidre agreed, offering up her own warm smile. "I feel sorry for Rodrick," she said.

Rose and Muriel were confused by her declaration. Muriel felt her face grow red with shame, as her mind raced for possible explanations. Was Deidre referring to the fact that Cora was not Rodrick's?

"What do ye mean?" Rose asked with a raised brow. She looked angry and fully prepared to put Deidre in her place.

"Och! When that wee lass is old enough to discover the lads and the lads take notice of her?" Deidre giggled as she held up a cup of milk for her son to drink from. "Och! Rodrick's hair will turn white with worry!"

Relief washed over Muriel. There had been nothing harsh in her sympathy for Rodrick. Even Rose looked relieved.

"Our men will be home before we realize it. And I reckon 'twill no' take long for any of us to wonder why we missed them," she said cheekily.

Deidre giggled in agreement.

Muriel, while she understood the playfulness in Rose's comment, could not believe there would ever be a time she would find Rodrick bothersome. She loved him too much.

FOR THE FIRST TIME IN MONTHS, MURIEL WAS ALONE IN HER BED. SHE missed having Rodrick sleeping next to her, the sound of his gentle breaths, and even the feel of snuggling up against him. On this cold spring night, she put Cora in the bed with her in hopes it would take away some of the loneliness. Quietly, she prayed that God would bring Rodrick back to her soon and without injury.

She took a measure of comfort in knowing the *sgian dubh* Rodrick had given her was tucked under her pillow. Though she seriously doubted there would be a need for it this night. After all, she was safely ensconced inside the walls of the keep.

Rodrick had promised to teach her how to defend herself. 'Twas something they would begin upon his return. She looked forward to learning how to not only use the *sgian dubh* but also how to use her own hands if ever she was put in such a situation. 'Twas doubtful such an occurrence would ever happen, but 'twould still make her feel more assured, and even safer.

With her babe next to her, she listened to the sounds of the fire crackling softly in the brazier as the spring winds howled and blew against their little home. *Home.* My, how her life had changed since Rodrick walked into it. Muriel felt safe here and even fulfilled. Rodrick and Cora had brought a measure of happiness into her life that at one time, she was certain she could never attain.

Caressing Cora's plump cheek with the back of her index finger, Muriel could not help but smile. "I love ye, me wee sweet babe. Yer da and I shall always protect ye, no matter the cost." 'Twas a declaration and promise she had heard Rodrick make to the babe since the day she was born. And 'twas one Muriel fully intended to keep as well. "As long as there is a breath left in me, I shall make certain no one ever does to you what was done to me. And yer da will do the same."

Feeling confident in that promise, Muriel finally drifted off to sleep, thinking of her future with Rodrick. *"I shall be a good wife to ye, Rodrick"* she promised herself.

Realizing just how much she did in fact love her husband, she made a decision. As soon as Rodrick returned, she was going to give herself to him fully. Oddly enough, thinking about it did not set her heart to pounding with fear. Nor did it make her feel disgusted.

Rodrick was a good, kind, gentle soul. Undoubtedly, their joining together would be much like him: sweet and gentle and tender.

She drifted off to sleep, with visions of her husband holding her in his arms, of him whispering his affection and adoration for her. She would finally give him the words that she'd been holding on to for far too long. She loved him, and it was high time he knew it. Thinking of Rodrick's arms wrapped around her, and how he would respond when she finally told him, made her feel warm and at peace.

At some point — whether 'twas hours or only moments later, it mattered not — she was torn from her peaceful slumber by a hand clasped tightly over her mouth. Terror enveloped her to the point she could not move or even try to scream.

"If ye try to scream, we will kill yer babe first, then ye."

The croft was bathed in muted darkness, with only the embers from the brazier to light the small space. Muriel didn't know the man who had his hand over her mouth and a cold blade pressed against her throat.

Her heart pounded against her breast as panic set in. *Cora!* She screamed silently, frozen with fear and dread.

"Ye do as we say, and ye both shall live, aye?"

She couldn't see his face, for 'twas too dark. Naught more than a terrifying silhouette, a black shadow in the night. Unable to speak, she begged and pleaded silently for mercy for her daughter.

Someone else was in the hut with them, another dark shadow who bent over the bed and lifted Cora up and away. *Nay! Nay! Nay!* Muriel screamed silently. *Do no' hurt me babe!*

"Nod yer head if ye understand," the voice scolded.

Muriel nodded her head rapidly as she watched the man carry her babe into darkness.

"Good," he said. "Now, ye are goin' to get up and ye are comin' with us. Mangus will be holdin' yer babe until we are far away from this keep. Ken that he will no' think twice about plungin' his dirk into yer wee one's heart if ye do anythin' to keep us from escape. Nod yer head again if ye understand."

Again, she nodded her head. There was no doubt in her mind this man meant every word he spoke.

Slowly, he removed his hand from her face and stood to his full height. "Come now," he said. "We have no time to dally!"

Muriel all but flung herself from the bed, looking around the hut frantically for her child. Save for herself and this man, the hut was empty. Tears fell down her cheeks as white-hot fury and dread filled her heart. "Where is me babe?" she asked, choking on sobs.

"Mangus has her safe and sound," the man replied. "Now, get yer cloak and shoes." He grabbed her arm and began to pull her toward the door. "And remember, yer child's life rests solely in yer hands."

Good lord! She cried silently. *I forgot about the sgian dubh!*

THE WIND, STRONG AND AT TIMES VIOLENT, DROWNED OUT THE SOUND of their footsteps. Walking in the dark shadows along the wall, they took Muriel to the rear of the wall, to a small door. Next to that door lay one of the McLaren men, sprawled out on his back. Blood oozed from a gaping wound on the side of his head. Blank, lifeless eyes stared up at the night sky. There would be no time to mourn the loss of an innocent young man.

Her captor quietly pushed open the door before pulling Muriel through.

CHAPTER SIXTEEN

Moments later, they were standing in near complete darkness. He grabbed her arm forcefully once again as he shoved her along. With all her might, she wanted to scream, to call out for help. But she knew the moment she did that, a man she'd never met would be driving a dirk into her daughter's heart.

Muriel could not think clearly for she was too overcome with terror and dread. Blood rushed in her ears as they made their way across the small clearing and into the woods. Once, she tripped over her own feet and fell face first into the wet earth. She swallowed back her tears and the urge to groan. When the strange, angry man pulled her back to her feet, she was beset with memories of the year before when she'd been sold and taken to Captain Wallace's ship.

The wind soon blew the clouds away from the moon, and the earth was bathed in its white light. Muriel found no comfort in the brightness. Soon, she was being pulled along through the dense forest and bramble bushes. Limbs tore at her skin and her cloak. Her captor was not concerned with her safety or wellbeing, only that she remain quiet.

They seemed to walk a mile or more before they came upon a

small clearing. There, she saw at least a dozen men on horseback, but they were naught more than black shadows and shapes. "Where be my babe?" she whispered fearfully.

The brutish man said nothing as he tossed her atop a horse before climbing up behind her. Soon, they were all riding farther and farther away from the place she had called home.

"Where be my babe?" she asked once again, a bit more forcefully this time. She was growing angrier by the moment. They had stolen into the keep, into her home and were taking her to God only knew where. And they had her babe, threatening to kill Cora should she do anything wrong.

The man behind her squeezed her tightly around her waist. "Wheest, or neither ye nor yer babe will make it to our destination."

"I want my babe!" she exclaimed in a harsh whisper.

A moment later, she felt the cold steel of a dirk pressed against her throat. "I meant what I said," he ground out. "Ye talk again before I give ye permission, and *I* will force ye to watch as we kill yer daughter."

JUST BEFORE THE SUN BEGAN TO PEEK OUT OVER THE HORIZON, MURIEL was much relieved to hear her daughter cry. Crying meant Cora was still alive and well. Thankfully, they gave the babe over to her. Tearfully, she took her daughter into her arms and held her tightly, but the babe continued to cry.

"Shut the babe up," her captor ground out.

Muriel took the chance of a brief glance back at the cruel man. He appeared to be at least forty, and he was just as foul looking as she had imagined. A slight scar on one cheek, dark brown, furious looking eyes were staring straight ahead. He and the others wore plaids with colors she did not recognize.

Using her cloak for some measure of privacy, she lowered the bodice of her nightdress to allow Cora to nurse. Her mind raced to find some logical reason as to why they'd been stolen away in the middle of the night, but she came up empty. None of this made a lick of sense.

They were not part of Captain Wallace's crew, of that much she was certain. These men were warriors, but just which clan they belonged to, she couldn't begin to guess. Mayhap this was all a terrible mistake and they didn't mean to kidnap her. What if they had been coming for Rose? 'Twas quite possible. Kidnapping a chief's wife or their children and holding them for ransom was a common occurrence amongst the Highland clans. Mayhap if she told them who she was, they would realize their mistake and return her at once.

"Me name be Muriel MacElroy, wife of Rodrick," she began.

"I ken who ye be," the man said.

"But why have ye taken me?" she asked, glancing at him over her shoulder. "Me husband can ill afford to pay a ransom," she explained.

He grunted but refused to look at her or offer a reply.

"I should verra much like an explanation as to why ye drug me out of me home in the middle of the night," she said, her words clipped and biting.

He grunted again. "I will let Fergus MacDonald explain it to ye."

An unprecedented terror consumed her to her bones. *Fergus? Nay! That cannot be!* A hundred questions flashed in her mind. Why? Why would he come after her now? What could he possibly want from her? Why would he take such a risk as this? Unfortunately, she could find no answers, at least none that did not involve her being made his slave again.

Tears welled in her eyes. Unable to stop them, she left them fall, along with any hope of ever having a normal kind of existence.

FURY UNLIKE ANYTHING HE HAD EVER EXPERIENCED BEFORE BURNED deep in Rodrick the Bold's gut. White-hot fury drowned out the voices of the messengers who brought the news. Someone had stolen into their keep and taken his wife and daughter.

"We found Callum dead late last night," the young man was telling him and Ian. "We do no' ken how in the bloody hell they got inside the keep!"

Ian, almost as equally furious as Rodrick, but for entirely different reasons, was pacing back and forth. They were standing in a small clearing, halfway between their keep and the Randall holding. The plan had been to hide, to lie in wait in the hopes of catching a few unsuspecting Randalls and *questioning* them about their previous attack on their border.

"Bloody hell!" he ground out. "What do ye mean ye have no idea how they got inside our walls?"

The young man paled and seemed to shrink before his laird and chief. Behind him, the other messenger took a few steps back.

"It doesn't bloody matter *how* they got in!" Rodrick bellowed. "They have taken me wife and daughter!"

Terrified, the two young men knew not what to do or say at the moment. They stood on weak legs and held their tongues.

Furiously, Rodrick stormed across the small clearing toward *Caderyn.* There was no reason for Ian to ask him where he was going.

"Wait!" Ian called out to him as he raced to catch up to him. "What if it was the Randalls who took them?" he asked Rodrick.

Rodrick didn't pause for even a brief moment. "If it was the Randalls, we would have seen them," he replied as he took to his horse.

That much was true. The Randalls would have had to come through this part of their lands to get from the Mackintosh keep to their own.

"Mount up!" Ian called out to the rest of their men. Soon, they were tearing across the countryside heading back to their keep.

Ian pulled his horse alongside Rodrick's. "Hopefully we will find more answers upon our return," he said. Even he didn't believe his own words. But if anyone understood what Rodrick was going through, 'twas he. His sweet Rose had been kidnapped by the Bowie's more than a year ago. 'Twas the single most difficult time of his entire life.

"We will find them," he told Rodrick.

Rodrick didn't so much as grunt or look his way.

A FEW HOURS LATER, THEY WERE TEARING THROUGH THE GATES OF THE Mackintosh keep. Rodrick slid from *Caderyn* before the animal had come to a complete stop. Men and women alike came rushing up to him and Ian.

"Laird!" Phillip McLaren called out as he ran across the yard to meet them. "They be heading' north!"

Rodrick stopped dead in his tracks. The long ride home had done nothing to quell his fury. Ian came to stand beside him.

Out of breath, Phillip began to explain what they knew. "As soon as we found Callum dead, we searched the entire keep and all the huts. We soon discovered Muriel and the babe were missin'."

A dull ache began to form behind Rodrick's left eye. "We ken me wife and daughter are gone!" he yelled.

Nonplussed, Phillip continued to explain. "As soon as we kent they were missin', I sent men out in search of them." He reached into his sporran then and pulled out a bit of brown wool. "One of the men found this in the woods north of here." He handed the fabric to Rodrick.

"Be it Muriel's?" Ian asked.

Rodrick nodded his head. "Aye," he ground out. Dread and anger blended together as he rubbed the fabric betwixt his fingers.

"I had the men continue to search," Phillip told them. "We suspect they got at least a three-hour head start on us."

Rodrick glanced at the man, thankful he had shown some common sense. Phillip might not be the best of fighting men, but he was showing promise. The fact he had not simply waited for orders elevated him in Rodrick's eyes.

"Rodrick, we shall gather supplies and head out," Ian said before turning to Phillip. "We'll need fresh horses," he said to Phillip.

"We have them waitin' already," Phillip said. "As well as food and more men."

Ian slapped the man on his back with his palm. "Good," he replied before turning his attention back to Rodrick. "We can no' afford to take all the men away from the keep," he said.

Rose came pushing through the crowd then. Her eyes were red from crying. "Ian!" she called out to him. He drew her in for a warm embrace.

"Rodrick," she said as she pulled away. "I be so sorry!"

Rodrick could only offer her a curt nod. Words were lodged in his throat, along with bile and worry. "Ye will get them back," Rose told him as she placed a hand on his arm. "I ken ye will."

He would get her back or he'd die trying.

CHAPTER SEVENTEEN

Muriel had not eaten a thing since the night she'd been taken from her home. She doubted she could have eaten even the tiniest morsel of food, for her stomach was filled with too much fear and dread.

The ferry ride across the sea to Skye had been tumultuous, to say the least. A storm had come in, rocking the ferry back and forth violently. She clung to Cora with all her might and prayed. She prayed for their safety, but mostly, she prayed that Rodrick would get to her in time.

Rodrick would come for her. This she knew to her marrow.

The only worry she possessed was that they would not figure out in time just who had taken her or where they were going. But she knew he would come for her. That thought was the only thing that kept her moving forward. Rodrick would not forsake her. He would not forget about her.

'Twas midday by the time the ferry landed on Skye. There was no reason to ask where they were going. The questions that loomed large were 'why?' and 'for what purpose??' What could Fergus possibly want from her? He'd already sold her once before. He and Anthara had washed their hands of her a year ago. Why on earth were they coming back into her life now?

On weak legs, cold and drenched from the journey, she followed her captors through the small village. As soon as Fergus and Anthara's home came into her line of vision, her dread intensified to the point she felt light headed. This had been her hell on earth for many months. A hell she had thought she'd left behind. Now, she was back again. Muriel could not help but feel terrified and helpless. But this time, she was not without hope.

Rodrick will come for me, she told herself. *He will kill ye all.* Knowing this tiny fact bolstered her resolve and determination.

Soon, they were stepping over the threshold of the back door, returning her to the man who had been her tormentor and abuser.

Ye will no' win again.

FERGUS MACDONALD JUMPED FROM HIS SEAT BY THE FIRE AND WALKED toward Muriel. His smile might have fooled a complete stranger, but Muriel knew it for what it was: naught more than a mask to cover the face belonging to a most cruel and sadistic man.

"Muriel," he said, still smiling as if she were a long, lost friend. He dismissed all but one of the men. The one who had taken her from her bed remained behind, standing near the door, quietly observing.

A year ago, she would have felt small and weak and very afraid in the presence of these men, but not this day. She was a different person now: a wife and mother. Instead of trembling, she gave Fergus a cold, hard stare and drew from deep within. Pushing her shoulders back and lifting her chin, she refused to take her eyes off him.

"'Tis good to see ye again," Fergus said as he retook his chair.

"I can no' say the same to ye," she told him bluntly.

Her response surprised him. Cocking his head to one side, he studied her for the briefest of moments. With a nod toward the bundle in her arms, he said, "I would like to meet me daughter."

Grinding her teeth, Muriel held Cora even closer. "She is no' yers.

She belongs to me husband, Rodrick. And I want to be returned to him immediately."

Fergus raised a brow dubiously. "Well, now, I have ciphered it all out, Muriel and I ken fer a fact the babe be mine."

"Nay," she said, trying to calm the worry growing in her belly. "She belongs to Rodrick." As far as she was concerned, Rodrick *was* Cora's father.

Disgusted, Fergus pursed his lips together and gave a slow shake of his head. "We both ken that is no' the truth."

Ignoring his statement, Muriel said, "Release me and ye might live another day."

He began to laugh then, throwing his head back and chuckling heartily like the fool that he was. "Och! Muriel!" he said after a time, "just who do ye think will be takin' me life?"

Tilting her head ever so slightly, she glowered at him. "Rodrick."

He stood then, shaking his head slowly, looking as though he held the greatest of secrets. "Ye mean the man I have locked away in me da's dungeon?"

NAY! MURIEL CRIED SILENTLY. *NAY, THAT CAN NO' BE!*

Knowing Fergus's propensity for lying, she refused to believe him. *He is just tryin' to scare ye to get ye to do what he wants.* "Ye lie," she accused.

"Do I?" he asked.

Although her stomach was drawing into knots, she refused to give up hope just yet. "Ye do," she insisted. Thinking quickly, hoping to catch him up in his own false words, she said, "If ye have him, then show him to me."

"Nay, I do no' think so," Fergus said, his smile gone now.

"Then bring to me the ring Rodrick wears around his neck," she challenged.

Fergus looked to the man who had been standing quietly near the door. "Roger? Was Rodrick the Bold wearin' a ring around his neck when ye captured him?"

Roger took a step forward and smiled deviously at Muriel. "Nay, I do no' think he was, m'laird. But then, he put up a good fight. Until the blade of me brother's sword near gutted him."

Muriel sucked in a deep breath as she took a step back. *Nay! Nay! Nay! That can no' be!*

"He be quite injured," Fergus said. "He *might* live if he had a healer."

The prospect of losing Rodrick was almost too much to bear. Tears welled in Muriel's eyes, her resolve quickly fading.

In a few short strides, Fergus was standing so close to her she could feel his breath on her face. "Now, if ye were to cooperate and do as I say, then I will allow a healer to tend to yer husband's wounds."

Muriel felt light-headed and terrified all at once. If what he said was true, she could not chance angering Fergus. The image of Rodrick bleeding to death in a cold dungeon made her feel sick to her stomach. But if what he said was naught more than a lie? Either way, she had to either buy her husband's freedom and life or give him time to get here. But what could Fergus possibly want from her that would justify him kidnapping her, her babe, and possibly killing her husband? Any answer that came to mind terrified her.

Fergus gave her very little time to think. "Ye see, me da wants to take away me inheritance. All I need do to keep it is to produce an heir. It matters no' who the mother be, just that I have fathered one."

FERGUS WANTED HER BABE.

Too paralyzed with the realization, Muriel could neither cry nor even speak. All she could do was to look at him in abject terror. *He wants me babe.*

"I care no' a whit about the child, ye ken. But I have to prove to me da that I have fathered one," he explained.

"Ye're mad," she finally ground out. "Ye will have to take this babe from me cold dead hands!"

He laughed at her distress and horror. "That could be arranged," he said. "But I fear me da will want proof from ye that 'twas I who fathered yer bastard child."

Bile rose in her throat. He was quite serious.

"Me da returns on the morrow. Ye and I shall go to him then and present the babe to him as mine. As soon as ye have convinced him of the truth — that 'twas I who fathered the babe— I shall have a healer tend to yer husband's injuries and set the both of ye free. If ye do a verra good job, I might even let ye take the brat back home with ye."

Her head swam with trepidation and outrage as words lodged in her throat. Fergus was as insane as the day was long; there was no doubt of it now.

"Do ye understand what I be askin' of ye?"

Before she could curse him to the devil, Anthara walked into the room.

"Ah! Sweetin'!" Fergus said to his wife. "Look what I have fer ye!"

Anthara paused just inside the doorway, her eyes fixed solely on the babe in Muriel's arms.

Fergus leaned in to whisper into Muriel's ear. "Anthara believes she will be keepin' the babe to raise as her own. Do no' let her think otherwise, else I shall order Rodrick killed and ye as well. Do ye understand?"

The tears fell as Anthara approached. "The wet-nurse will no' be here until the morrow," she said as she began to pry Cora from Muriel's arms.

"Nay!" Muriel cried out. "Leave her be!"

Roger grabbed Muriel about the waist as Anthara and Fergus pried her daughter from her arms. "Nay! Give her back to me!"

As soon as Anthara had a good hold on the babe, she turned to walk away, looking gleefully happy. Fergus grabbed Muriel's arm and twisted it behind her back. "Quiet!" he whispered harshly. "Or I swear I shall have Roger here cut yer throat."

Muriel's heart began to shatter as she watched Anthara walk away.

Fergus continued his tight hold on her arm, but Muriel ignored the pain. It was nothing compared to the thought of never seeing her child again.

Yanking harder, Fergus began to speak again. His voice was deep, angry, and menacing. "Ye do as I say or ye shall never lay yer eyes on yer babe again," he warned her. "Yer husband's life and yer own rests solely in yer hands."

Yer life will rest in them too, ye bloody bastard.

CHAPTER EIGHTEEN

'T was another sleepless night for Muriel. She'd been locked into a tiny room down the hall from Anthara and Fergus, and away from Cora. The only time she was allowed to see the bairn was when 'twas time to feed her. She clung to every moment with her babe, hoping and praying their ordeal would soon be over. Under the close, watchful eyes of Anthara, Muriel fed her daughter, all the while she imagined the different ways she could take Anthara and Fergus's lives.

If what Fergus said was true, her husband could very well be dying. The image of him alone, on the cold floor of a dungeon, bleeding to death, tore at her heart. Rodrick needed her. He needed her to be strong, to do whatever she could to gain his freedom. There was no doubt in her mind that he would do the same for her. That was if what Fergus had told her was the truth.

With a guard at her door and another under her window, any thought of escape was futile. So she remained quiet, refusing to speak to any of them.

Muriel would do exactly as Fergus wanted only to gain their freedom. If Rodrick was injured, she would see him fully recovered, no matter the cost. And as soon as he was better, they would come back and lay an unholy siege to Fergus MacDonald's home. Images of his house burning to the ground with him and Anthara still inside were the only thing that brought her any measure of comfort.

Knowing she needed to eat in order to make milk for Cora, she managed to choke down a few bites of bread and meat that morning. Her stomach was tied in knots of worry and dread and heartache.

As soon as Muriel was done nursing Cora, Anthara took her away. Muriel's arms felt cold and empty and it took every ounce of courage not to scream and rail against the woman. The moment Anthara left the room, Fergus stepped inside.

"We shall be leavin' shortly, fer me father's keep," he told her as he stared out the small window. "Ye will admit to me da that I fathered yer babe."

It sickened her to admit to it whenever she was alone. To admit to it publicly would require more strength than she believed she possessed at the moment. Just thinking about it made her want to vomit.

"Ye will also tell him that ye've agreed to allow Anthara and I to raise the babe,"

Muriel shot to her feet. "Nay!" she cried.

Fergus held up a hand to stop her protests. "I have as much interest in raisin' yer babe as ye do in givin' her up. 'Tis only a wee bit of a lie, I can assure ye. I merely want me inheritance returned to me. Naught else."

Unable to believe a word that came out of his mouth, she pretended to believe him. Deep down, she knew Anthara would not give up Cora without a fight. But 'twas a fight Muriel found herself looking forward to.

"Ye have me word," Fergus told her.

She knew his word was as valuable as bird droppings.

I'll see ye all dead, she screamed silently. *Every last one of ye.*

FOG ROLLED IN AND BLANKETED THE ISLE IN A THICK, HEAVY MIST.

'Twas just after noonin' time before Fergus came to take Muriel to the MacDonald keep. He refused her pleas to keep her babe with her. Instead, Anthara held the babe as if she were her very own during the journey north.

Taking the well-worn path, they rode on horseback, with Fergus and Anthara leading the way. Muriel was surrounded by the Randall men as if she were a criminal they worried would try to escape. They couldn't have known she would rather die than leave this isle without her babe.

'Twas impossible to see more than a few feet in any direction. Though her heart was breaking, Muriel refused to shed any tears. She clung to her fervent belief that everything she was doing or about to do was for Rodrick and Cora. If he was injured, he needed a healer. If he wasn't, then certainly he would soon be coming for them. Either way, she knew she had to play along until she learned the truth.

Fergus called for her to be brought forward. It took a good deal of strength on her part not to reach out and push him off his horse.

"Remember, yer husband's life and that of yer babe rests solely in yer hands," Fergus reminded her. "As soon as ye tell me da that the babe is mine, I will send the healer to tend to yer husband."

There was no way for her to gauge his sincerity, for she knew him to be the cruelest sort of man.

"Tell me ye understand," Fergus said as he leaned over his mount.

"I understand," she replied harshly.

He nodded his approval before righting himself. "I hope fer yer sake as well as yer husband and babe's, that ye do no' forget me promise. I *will* kill all of ye if ye refuse to do what I tell ye."

Fergus ordered her back to the rear of the procession before she could make her own promise to him. *I will see* ye *dead someday.*

LIKE A GREAT, GIANT MONSTER EMERGING FROM THE NETHERWORLD, the MacDonald keep came into view. Materializing through the dense fog, it stood on a grassy knoll overlooking Loch Lethian. Behind the massive stone wall was an outcropping of ancient rocks jutting up from the earth like unearthly fingers reaching from a grave. Muriel could not help but shiver in fear at the sight.

Young men seemed to appear from nowhere to take their horses. One of her captors pulled Muriel from her mount with little effort or kindness. Soon, she was being pushed up the steps and into the keep.

They passed under a murder wall, up a small flight of stairs, and into the large gathering room. 'Twas filled with all manner of people, there, she assumed, to seek an audience with their laird and chief.

There was no mistaking which of the men who sat at the long, high table, was the Chief of the MacDonald Clan. The man sitting in the ornately carved, high backed chair had to be Walter MacDonald.

A thick, long beard covered most of his face. 'Twas his crystal blue eyes that made her blood run cold. Not as possessed and demonic as his son's. Nay, these eyes told a thousand stories of battles fought and won, of strength and power. He was not a man to be toyed with nor his patience tested.

At the moment, he looked bored and perturbed as he listened to a man complaining about one of his neighbors.

Muriel paid little attention to the proceedings. Looking about the room, she hoped and prayed she'd find Rodrick hiding in the shadows, ready to pounce like a wild cat o'mountain in order to gain their freedom.

Her hope faded when she did not see him. Although she did not see him, she could feel his presence. He *was* here, her heart screamed. But not as her rescuer. 'Twas then an uneasiness fell over her, for she soon began to realize Fergus had not been lying. Somewhere below, in the dark, cold, and filthy recesses of this keep, was her husband. More likely than not, he was dying a slow, agonizing death.

With that realization, her resolve to save him as he had saved her began to grow. There was no guarantee that Fergus would keep his word. There was a strong possibility that no matter what she did this day, she and Rodrick could very well end up dead. That would leave Cora to be raised by two demented individuals.

Muriel's determination increased by the moment. There was no way on God's earth she would allow her daughter to be raised by these deranged people. Nay, she would do whatever she must to see that didn't happen.

She was pulled from her despondent reverie by the sound of Fergus's voice. "'Tis time."

FERGUS LED MURIEL UP TO THE HIGH TABLE, SHOWING GREAT CONCERN for her wellbeing. 'Twas just another of his lies. If she dropped dead now, it wouldn't matter in the least to him. Muriel and Cora were simply a means to an end.

He offered a short bow of respect and a warm smile to his father.

Walter looked just as bored and perturbed with Fergus as he had the previous clansman. He toyed with his beard before taking a glance at Muriel.

"Da," Fergus began. "I have come to share me good news with ye."

Walter grunted his displeasure. "And what might that be?"

"I have an heir," he replied as he turned to wave Anthara forward. His statement piqued Walter's interest. The man sat upright in his chair, looking confused.

Muriel found Anthara's countenance odd. She didn't come forward with her head held high or her usual smug expression. Nay, she kept her head down and looked meek and mild. Muriel resisted the urge to laugh.

"I was no' made aware Anthara was with child," Walter said as Anthara curtsied and smiled. He gave only a cursory glance toward her and the babe cradled in her arms.

Fergus's smile faded as he replaced it with a look of regret and sorrow. "'Tis with great shame that I admit the babe be no' Anthara's."

Walter's expression remained aloof. "I said ye must produce an heir, no' adopt one," he reminded his son.

"And I have," Fergus replied.

"How do I ken ye did no' just take a babe and try to pass it off as yer own?" Walter asked.

153

Fergus put a hand over his heart and feigned hurt. Turning to face Muriel, he said. "Durin' a moment of weakness more than a year ago I took to bed a young woman. The result of that encounter is the babe in me lovin' wife's arms."

Muriel drew her shoulders back but held her tongue. *A moment of weakness? An 'encounter'?* The man was mad.

Biting her tongue, she glared at Fergus.

Walter turned his focus to Muriel. "Who be ye?"

"I be Muriel MacElroy, wife to Rodrick MacElroy of the Mackintosh and McLaren clan," she answered proudly.

Walter raised a brow. "What game be this ye play?" he asked his son. "The lass be married. How do we ken the babe be no' his?"

Fergus appeared ready for the intense scrutiny and questioning. "She was in her seventh month when they married," he replied.

"Be this true?" Walter asked Muriel.

Suddenly her mouth felt as dry as a bone. "Aye." She nodded. Biting her tongue, she said nothing else for fear of reprisal from Fergus. She'd had firsthand experience with how quickly he could mete out punishment.

"Where be yer husband?" Walter asked.

Before she could reply *below stairs in yer dungeon,* Fergus stepped forward with another of his lies. "Unfortunately, he was unable to join us this day."

Walter remained skeptically quiet for a short time. "Did me son father yer bairn?"

As much as she wished to, she could not change that fact. "Aye," she replied stoically.

Another length of silence whilst Walter studied the three people standing before him. Unable to take the silence any longer, Fergus said, "Anthara and I will be raisin' the bairn as our own."

His words felt like a kick to her stomach. Stifling a repulsed gasp, she hung her head. *'Tis only temporary,* she promised herself. *Until ye can rescue Rodrick.* Her tears fell, and this time she cared not who saw them.

WALTER GRUNTED HIS DISPLEASURE DIRECTLY TOWARD HIS SON. PURSING his lips together, he glowered at Fergus. "Ye think this means ye will get yer inheritance now?" he asked.

Fergus shrugged his shoulders with indifference. "While it does no' matter to me," he began, "I do believe it be important fer me daughter. I will, of course, be officially declaring her mine, and givin' her me last name. 'Tis with great joy that Anthara and I will raise her together."

Feeling victorious, Fergus offered his father his warmest smile. The MacDonald's edict had declared Fergus must produce an heir. The legitimacy of the heir had never been mentioned nor discussed. Declaring the child his made her so. There could be no other argument against it.

While Walter appeared to not care one way or another, Fergus knew him better. Unfortunately, he would not be able to gloat, at least not yet. There would be time to celebrate his victory over his father later.

Blowing out a breath, his nostrils flaring, Walter glared at Fergus. "I believe me edict stated that ye and Anthara must produce an heir. I said nothin' about allowin' fer bastards or cast-offs."

Fergus was undeterred. "Nay, ye said naught of that. Nor do I believe ye mentioned me wife in yer edict. But the child still be mine."

Walter grunted. "Ye say ye care no' about yer monthly allowance or yer inheritance, aye?"

"I care only that me daughter be recognized as my child, as a MacDonald," Fergus said. 'Twas a full out lie and everyone in the room knew it. "I care only that me daughter is taken care of."

Walter slowly pushed away from the table and stood to his full height. He was even more imposing then. "Verra well then," he began. His countenance was that of a self-assured and exceedingly determined man. "Yer daughter — what be her name?"

Before Muriel could tell him, Anthara spoke up. "We will call her Burunild, after me mum."

Muriel could not protest or argue, at least not now. *Burunild?* 'Twas an awful name for babe as sweet as Cora.

Walter quirked one bushy eyebrow. "Burunild, then," he said. "Burunild shall be recognized as yer daughter and as a MacDonald."

Fergus stood tall and proud, puffing out his chest like a peacock.

"She shall receive *yer* inheritance and monthly allowance when she reaches the age of one and twenty or marries, whichever comes first."

Fergus's eyes bulged with astonishment. Cocking his head to one side he asked for clarification. "And as fer me? I have produced the heir ye required."

"Did ye by chance *read* the edict?" Walter asked.

Fergus stammered briefly. "I gave it a cursory glance," he admitted. "I relied on me brother, Gerome, to explain yer wishes to me."

Walter raised a brow in irritation. Turning to his steward — a man of middle age, average build, but strikingly bright red hair — he said, "Give me the original document."

The steward opened a leather case, old and worn with years of use, and began to search for the requested scroll. All the while, Fergus stood anxious and nervous. Sweat began to form across his brow.

It took only a few moments for the man to find the document in question. The steward pulled the scroll from the case and handed it to Walter. Walter held the document up for those in the room to see. Without pomp or ceremony, he removed the bit of leather binding and tossed it onto the table. Unrolling the paper, he began to read aloud. "Be it hereby known to one and all that I will disinherit my third born son, Fergus MacDonald, if he does no' produce an heir before the first of June in the year of our lord thirteen hundred fifty-seven. He must produce this heir with his legal and lawfully wedded wife, Anthara MacRay. If an heir is not born and livin' by that date, he will no longer receive the monthly allowance currently allotted to him, nor will he receive any inheritance upon me death. Dated this seventh day of September, the year of our lord thirteen hundred fifty-six, signed Walter MacDonald, chief of the clan MacDonald." When he finished, he tossed the scroll onto the table. "I believe the date for ye and Anthara to produce an heir has passed."

Fergus swallowed hard, his Adam's apple bobbing up and down. He curled his hands into tight fists. Even Anthara had the good sense to step away from him, for there was no denying his utter fury. Words were lodged firmly in his throat.

"I produced an heir," he finally managed to grind out. "I can no' help it if me wife be barren!"

Unfazed, Walter crossed his arms over his chest. "When ye were born, I had such high hopes fer ye. But somewhere along the way, ye became naught more than a severe disappointment to me. Ye have become lazy as well as cruel." Placing his palms on the table, he leaned over it slightly, speaking slowly, as if he did not want Fergus to mistake anything he was about to say. "Ye will no' get one more bit o' coin from me. No' one." Pausing only to make certain Fergus understood every word he said, Walter stood to his full height. "Now be gone with ye, and take yer barren wife, yer whore and bastard with ye." Without waiting for a response, Walter MacDonald turned and left the gathering room.

CHAPTER NINETEEN

Hidden in the shadows of the grand gathering room, Rodrick the Bold watched the scene unfolding before him. Like a coiled snake ready to strike its victim, he came close to doing just that as soon as Muriel admitted their babe was fathered by Fergus.

I be her father! He screamed silently. *Ye're naught more than a bloody son of a whore, Fergus MacDonald.*

When Fergus turned for a moment, Rodrick was able to get a better look at him.

This was the man who had tormented his wife? This scrawny, pale man with the dark eyes? *This* was the man who had come close to ruining Muriel to the point that she wanted to die? Rodrick was a full head taller and better built. He could snap the man's neck with little effort. His fingers fair itched in anticipation of doing just that.

Had Ian not been with him, who knew what he might have done. But Ian's good sense prevailed as he held Rodrick back with a simple touch on his arm. "Ye will get us all killed," he whispered calmly.

Rodrick watched in quiet fury as Muriel was forced to admit that Fergus had fathered her child. When she hung her head in shame, his gut tightened. Had Ian not been there to hold him back, he would have lunged forward and gutted Fergus in front of God, his father, and everyone else.

It took nerves of steel to wait patiently, to hide his face under the shadows of the cowl he wore, and not to pounce the moment Fergus walked by. To not reach out and pull his wife into his arms was one of the most painful things he had experienced in his life.

This was neither the time nor the place to seek his vengeance. But vengeance would be his. And soon.

MURIEL WAS STUNNED AT THE TURN OF EVENTS. IN FRONT OF GOD AND everyone, Walter MacDonald had disowned his son. Fissures of dread and terror raced up and down her spine. Who knew what Fergus would do now. If his past behavior was any indication…

She tried calling out to the MacDonald, to beg him to release her husband, but Fergus stopped her pleas. Grabbing her roughly by the arm, he began to pull her out of the gathering room.

"The healer," she pleaded. "I did everything ye asked. Please, send the healer to Rodrick."

Fergus held her arm tightly, his fingers digging into the tender flesh. "Wheesht!" he barked, looking around to make certain no one had heard her. He handed her off to one of his cohorts. "Get her out of here."

"Fergus?" Anthara said as she raced to keep up with him. Fergus ignored her, too infuriated with his father to behave with any kind of good sense.

Fergus called out to have their horses brought to them at once as they bounded down the stairs. Soon, they were spilling out of the keep and into the courtyard. The man continued to dig his fingers into Muriel's tender flesh. She should not have looked over her shoulder. Fergus's eyes were dark, nearly black, and filled with seething anger.

While they waited in the bailey for their horses, Fergus continued to fume.

"Fergus," Anthara whispered his name cautiously. "I get to keep the babe, aye?" There was so much hope in her eyes that Muriel almost felt sorry for her. *Almost.*

Fergus spun on his heels so quickly that Muriel was surprised he didn't fall over. "Shut. Up." His words were clipped, his tone harsh and spiteful.

"But I get to keep her, aye? Ye promised me." Tears were welling in her eyes as she held the babe so close to her breast that Muriel began to worry she might smother her.

Before Muriel could do anything to safely wrest Cora away, Fergus drew back his hand and slapped his wife, hard. She fell to the ground, but thankfully, she kept Cora safely tucked in a protective ball.

"I told ye to shut up!" Fergus ground out.

Muriel immediately went to Anthara and knelt beside her. The woman was not only hurt, but furious. She grew even more so when Muriel tried to take Cora away from her.

"Nay!" Anthara ground out. "She be *mine!*"

Two of the Randall men pulled Muriel away. As she kicked and screamed, Fergus took her face in one hand and squeezed hard. "If ye do no' shut up now, I will go inside and cut yer husband's throat meself," he ground out.

His hard fingers digging into her cheeks as well as his threat halted her protests. He squeezed again, one more time, before shoving her away as if he were disgusted with her. Turning his back, he called to one of his men. "Get me wife out of here."

"Where do ye wish us to take her?" the young man asked.

Seething, Fergus growled, "Home. Take her home!"

MURIEL WANTED TO SCREAM, TO CALL OUT FOR HELP, BUT WORRIED such a decision would be akin to signing her husband's death warrant. All she wanted in the world was to be back in her little home with Rodrick and Cora. At the moment, Rodrick lay dying in a dungeon and her daughter was being taken away by a madwoman.

In her heart, she knew Cora was safe, at least for now. Anthara had protected the babe, even when Fergus hit her and sent her to the cold, damp ground. At the moment, Cora was better off with Anthara.

Just outside the gates, Anthara and her guard turned southward, heading back to Portree. However, Fergus was leading their small group northward. Muriel shivered as panic began to rise. "Where are ye takin' me?" she asked.

Her question was met with cold silence, leaving her chilled to the bone with fear. "Where are we goin'?" she demanded once again.

"Wheesht!" the man next to her ground out. "Ye will find out when we get there."

Twisting around in her saddle, she looked back at the keep. If she tore away now, she could get back before the gates closed and beg for help. Realizing she could not take such a risk, knowing full well that Fergus would end up killing her and Rodrick, she turned back.

With her heart pounding against her chest, she tried reckoning out a solution: a way to save both her husband and her child. Surrounded by three MacDonald men as well as Fergus, she felt helpless. But she was not without hope.

Scanning the horizon, she wondered what her husband would do were he in the same predicament. *He would fight to the bitter end,* she thought. *He'd no' lay down and die.*

Across rough terrain they rode fast and hard. In unfamiliar territory, Muriel grew more and more distressed. Over a small, scraggly hill and down the other side, the land remained rough and jagged. When the wind picked up from the east, she caught the faint smell of the sea.

Nay, she screamed silently. Certainly they were not taking her to another ship, to be sold once again as a slave.

Then and there, she made a decision. Never again would she be afraid of nor fall victim to the likes of Fergus MacDonald.

For all she knew, Rodrick might already be dead. As much as it hurt to think of that possibility, she needed to remain strong and alive for Cora. She was not about to take the chance of leaving her child completely orphaned. For the first time in a very long while, Muriel chose to act instead of think.

Fergus was too busy fuming to pay any attention to what Muriel was or wasn't doing. In quiet rage, he plotted the best method to get even with his father. There were any number of ways to do it, of course. He knew how badly Gerome wanted to be the chief of their clan. Any fool with eyes could see it. Mayhap he could join forces with Gerome in unseating their father.

He could also begin rumors — none of them grounded in any kind of factual evidence — that Walter MacDonald was a traitor, or that he was not of sound mind, or that he liked to bugger young men. Aye, any of those things would work and each possessed a deviousness that held a certain amount of appeal.

But the idea he liked most was slicing his father's throat, watching the life drain from his body, then setting the keep on fire. And if by chance his two older brothers were inside? Well, then, Fergus would be the only one left to take the helm as the MacDonald chief. The image of his father's burning corpse rolling over in his grave because Fergus was at the helm brought a smile to his face. It could take some time, years perhaps, before he could manage it. 'Twas the only thing that kept him moving forward at the moment. That and what he planned to do with Muriel. If she thought he had been cruel to her before, she would believe those times naught more than a picnic along a quiet riverbank by comparison.

Aye, he had special plans for her.

He was so wrapped up in his own misery and scheming, he did not hear Thomas Randall until he called out a second time. Spinning around in his saddle, he could only watch in stunned surprise as Muriel rode away from them.

"Bloody hell!" he called out as he kicked the flanks of his horse and went after her.

Across the rocky terrain and up the jagged slope she went. Thomas and Peter were not far behind. Fergus was gaining speed and ground, cursing under his breath. If she by some chance got back to the MacDonald keep, then he was done for. If she got to his father and told him the truth, then everything he'd been working hard for these past months would be gone.

MURIEL COULDN'T HAVE KNOWN HER DECISION TO FLEE TURNED THE tables in her favor. Fergus's future now rested in her hands. Hands that were holding on to reins with a deathlike grip, hands that fair shook with unrivaled determination as well as fear.

Her only thought was getting away from Fergus and his men and back to the MacDonald keep. Anthara and her guard had a good head start. Muriel could only hope and pray that would play to her own advantage. Get to the keep, explain her situation, and plead for help to get her daughter back and a healer for Rodrick.

The sound of horses pounding across the ground, the men shouting and cursing, grew louder. She could feel the blood as it coursed through her veins, could feel it pounding in her ears. No matter what the men said, no matter what insults they hurled at her back, she wasn't about to stop.

As fast as the horse could take her, she rode up the rough rise, not daring to look back. Hunching over the neck of her mount, she clung on for dear life. Oh, how she wished she had the *sgian dubh* with her. Even if Rodrick hadn't taught her how to use it properly, she reckoned she could still do some amount of damage if she needed to.

Up the rise she went.

When she crested the top, the surprise at what she saw matched her momentum.

There were at least a dozen men on horseback racing towards her.

Stunned and terrified, she pulled hard on the reins of her horse. The brown steed cried out and reared. Muriel, unaccustomed to riding, did not know what to do and could not hold on. The horse reared again and sent her tumbling to the cold, hard earth.

RODRICK'S RELIEF AT SEEING HIS WIFE RIDING TOWARD HIM WAS SHORT lived.

He watched in abject horror as her horse reared once, then again. 'Twas as if the entire world slowed to a crawl as he saw his wife being hurled off the horse. Landing on her back, she did not move.

For the longest moment, his heart did not beat.

'Twas when he caught Ian and the other men racing toward her that he was finally propelled to move. "Muriel!" he yelled as he kicked his horse and raced towards her.

A moment later, her captors were coming over the rise and heading towards her. They took one look at the Mackintosh and McLaren men and pulled their horses to a halt. Just then, the object of all of Muriel's pain and heartache, and the one man Rodrick wanted the most in this world to see dead, came up and over the rise.

The fool did not even try to stop.

Fergus saw Muriel lying on the ground and headed right for her.

IAN WAS THE NEAREST TO FERGUS. WHEN HE SAW THE IDIOT'S intention, he kicked his horse into a full run. With sword drawn, he met Fergus before the man could trample Muriel into the earth. With the hilt of his sword and his mighty fist, Ian swung out. He hit his intended mark square in the jaw with such force, it sent Fergus tumbling to the ground.

He couldn't kill the man. Nay, he was saving that pleasure for Rodrick.

Pulling rein, Ian dismounted and stood over Fergus. "Move and ye die," he warned, as he pressed the tip of his blade to Fergus's chest. The man could not respond, for he was fighting hard to catch his breath.

Rodrick was off his mount and at Muriel's side. Carefully, he began looking for signs she still lived. His heart pounded ferociously against his chest as he tried to whisper her name. "Muriel, love," he choked. "Please wake up."

At the sound of her husband's voice, she opened her eyes. "Can't breathe," she said.

Relief washed over him like the waters of *Mealt Falls* . His breath came out in a great whoosh as he lifted her head into his arms. She'd had the wind knocked from her lungs. He saw no sign of blood, which made him feel even more relieved.

Muriel lifted one arm slowly and grabbed hold of his arms. "Kill him," she whispered.

He needed no more encouragement than that.

RODRICK LEFT MURIEL TO THE GOOD CARE OF ONE OF THE McLAREN men. Standing slowly, he withdrew his sword and went to stand beside Fergus MacDonald. The men who had been riding with Fergus had more intelligence than he would have given them credit for. They had dismounted — encouraged, he supposed — by five of the men who had ridden with him and Ian. The Randall men were now on their knees, divested of their swords and other weapons. Both of them had broken out into a cold sweat and were looking up at him nervously. He'd leave them be for now. He had more important matters to attend to.

Standing over Fergus MacDonald, he shook his head in disgust. Closer now than when they'd been in the MacDonald keep, Rodrick was even less impressed with the man. He was naught more than a weak, sadistic puppet.

Catching his breath, Fergus laughed sinisterly. "I take it," he said between breaths, "ye be Rodrick the Bold."

Rodrick cocked his head to one side. "Aye, I am. And ye be the bloody son of a whore named Fergus MacDonald."

Another laugh and a nod from Fergus as he slowly rolled over and struggled to his feet. "Aye, that be me," he said.

Rodrick remained quiet as he studied the man closely.

165

"I take it ye'll be wantin' to kill me now," Fergus said as he finally began to catch his breath. Resting his hands on his knees, he bent at the waist, taking in slow, deep breaths.

"Aye, I will be killin' ye this day," Rodrick replied. His voice was calm, steady, and his tone was unmistakably blunt. He was, at the moment, trying to decide the best way to do it. The manner that would give him the most satisfaction. Slicing his throat? Gutting him and leaving his entrails on the ground? Hanging? In the end, he supposed it didn't matter. Fergus MacDonald would still be dead.

Fergus chuckled once again, still bent over. He looked up at Rodrick and shook his head. "Forgive me," he began, "if I do no' wish to go down without a fight!"

Before he finished speaking, he'd lunged at Rodrick and caught him off guard. He'd hit him with enough force that it knocked Rodrick backward, sending them both tumbling to the ground. Rodrick's sword fell from his hand and slid across the earth.

Fergus may have seemed scrawny and without any strength, but he had enough to knock Rodrick down. However, he should not have taken too much false pride or hope in his action.

Rodrick lifted his legs and kicked out, summarily dislodging and tossing Fergus away as if he were naught but a pup. In one fluid motion, he was back on his feet and retrieving his sword.

Fergus struggled back to his knees. "Ye may kill me," he said, "but it does no' change the fact that the bastard child is mine."

Infuriated, Rodrick gritted his teeth. "She is no' a bastard. She has a name." His words were clipped, his tone cold yet furious.

"Aye, she does!" Fergus laughed. "Her name be Burunild MacDonald," he said before spitting on the ground.

Rodrick could take no more. With his sword in both hands, he lifted it over his shoulder. With all his strength, he brought the sword down hard, slicing across Fergus MacDonald's throat. Blood spurted from the gaping wound. Fergus's eyes grew wide with incredulity.

"Nay," Rodrick said before bringing the sword across Fergus's neck from the opposite direction. "Her name be Cora MacElroy."

Fergus MacDonald teetered for a few moments, as the blood and life drained from his body. Moments later, he fell onto his side, his once sadistic and cruel eyes now lifeless.

MURIEL HAD WATCHED THE ENTIRE SCENE UNFOLD BEFORE HER EYES.

Frozen on her knees, she saw her husband slice his blade across Fergus's throat, once, twice, and yet again. The third strike effectively severed Fergus's head from his neck. The head fell to the ground with a sickening thud and rolled back and forth for what seemed an extraordinarily long time. Finally, it came to rest; the dark yet lifeless eyes seemed to be staring directly at her.

Her stomach roiled. She had never seen anything even remotely like it before. Finally, she could take no more. Turning her head away she buried it in the nearest chest she could find, caring not who it belonged to.

"Wheesht," he said as he patted her back. She knew he was a McLaren, but that was all she could remember at the moment.

It seemed a long time passed as she wept against the McLaren man's chest. 'Twas a blend of relief and disgust. Briefly, she wondered if God would be displeased with her for feeling so much solace in knowing Fergus MacDonald was dead. Later, much later, she'd do her best to make peace with Him. For now, her emotions were too high, her relief too grand.

It was finally over.

Fergus MacDonald was dead. He could never hurt her again. Nor could he hurt Cora.

Cora! Saying her babe's name in her head began to draw her out of the dense fog. "Cora," she whispered, her panic beginning to return in leaps and bounds.

Rodrick was soon at her side, helping her to her feet. "Wheesht," he whispered. "Cora be fine."

"Nay!" she argued, grabbing his arms for balance and strength. "Anthara took her!"

Rodrick drew her into his chest and kissed the top of her head. "Anthara did no' get far," he told her. "Our men went after them."

She drew very little reassurance from that knowledge. "But ye do no' understand! Anthara is determined to keep her as her own!" she said as she drew her head back. As if seeing him for the first time, she said, "Why are ye no' dead? Fergus said he had ye in the dungeon, that ye were mortally wounded!"

Rodrick smiled down at her. "'Twas a lie, Muriel. I be as right as rain."

'Twas all too much. She fell against his chest, wrapping her arms around him. "I thought ye were dyin' or already dead!" she cried. "I had to save our daughter. Please, believe me."

Hugging her tightly, Rodrick said, "Lass, do no' fash yerself over it. I ken what ye did and why. Come now, let us go get our daughter and go home."

Home.

A year ago that word meant naught to her. But now? Today? It meant everything.

CHAPTER TWENTY

The Mackintosh men were waiting for them, just as Rodrick and Ian had planned. They had successfully gotten the babe back from a very upset and rather insane Anthara MacDonald. Later, they would recount the story to Rodrick, of how the woman had screamed like a banshee, had fought tooth and nail, clawing at their faces as they took the babe from her arms. They left her and her guard alongside the road to Portree.

But for now, they oohed and ahed over the tiny babe, doing their best to keep her from crying. The poor thing was undoubtedly hungry, but all they had to offer her was dried beef. Somehow, they didn't think her mother would appreciate them giving the toothless babe dried beef or bits of apples.

They were mightily glad to see Ian, Rodrick, Muriel and the others, bounding down the road. Rodrick had his arms wrapped around his wife. Muriel could not wait for the horse to stop before she was scurrying off its back.

"Cora!" she exclaimed as she raced forward and grabbed her from the arms of William Mackintosh.

Between kisses for her babe, she thanked the men repeatedly.

Rodrick stood behind her now, just as glad to see his daughter as her mother was.

"Thank ye," he told the men surrounding them. "I - we - will never be able to repay ye."

"Bah!" Callum said with a shake of his head. "Ye would have done the same for any one of us."

Cora began to cry rather loudly. It had been hours since last she'd eaten.

Rodrick helped Muriel to a quiet spot and set her down on a felled log. "Ye rest here and feed our daughter, aye?" he said before kissing first the top of Muriel's head, then Cora's. He started to walk away when Muriel stopped him.

"Where are ye goin'?" she asked, sounding afraid.

"Ye feed our babe. I have one more thing to do."

"Nay!" she cried out over the waling cries of her babe. "Ye can no' mean to leave me now!"

Kneeling before her he said, "Wheesht, Muriel. I promise, I will no' be gone long. Ian will be with ye, as well as the rest of the men. I shall meet ye at the ferry in less than an hour."

Tears pooled and fell. "Please, Rodrick, do no' leave me."

He smiled warmly and placed a gentle palm on her cheek. "I swear to ye, where I be goin' is no' dangerous."

He left her then, sitting on a wide log, looking sadder than he'd ever seen her. But there was something important he needed to do.

STANDING NEAR THEIR HORSE, RODRICK SPOKE TO IAN. "I WILL TAKE Callum with me," he said. "Please, see me wife safely to the ferry. And ye leave, with or without me."

"And where might ye be goin'?" Ian asked as he rubbed his chin with his hand.

"I have to deliver Fergus's head."

Ian did not ask another question. He watched as Rodrick strode to Ian's horse. Hanging there, in a sack, was Fergus's head. Rodrick untied it from Ian's mount before tying it to the saddle of his own. "No matter what happens, ye see me wife and daughter safely home."

Ian let out a heavy breath. "Aye, ye have me word. But promise me two things."

Rodrick gave him a nod. "What might that be?"

"That ye do no' start any wars and that ye come back to yer wife and child."

Rodrick nodded his head again but said not a word as he and Callum rode away.

RODRICK AND CALLUM LET THEMSELVES INTO ANTHARA MACDONALD'S home. No one had answered their repeated knocks at the door. They could hear a woman crying and the sound of things being thrown against the walls within.

They found her in a small room just off the hallway. Anthara had only that moment thrown a candlestick at the wall next to the hearth when they stepped inside. There were bits of broken furniture and pottery scattered about the room. She'd picked up a small table when she turned and saw them standing in the doorway.

Fury filled her eyes. "Go away!" she screamed at them.

Most women would have made an inquiry as to their identities.

"I be Rodrick MacElroy, husband to Muriel MacElroy," he said, ignoring her demand.

Recognition was quick to set in. Gritting her teeth together, she screamed, "She took my babe!" In the next instant, she was hurling the small table at them. Callum stepped forward and grabbed it before it could strike either one of them. Carefully, he placed the table on the floor near his feet.

"Cora be no' yer babe," Rodrick told her pointedly.

"Yes she is! She be mine and Fergus's! That whore ye call yer wife is no' fit to raise a dog!" Her eyes were filled with unsuppressed rage and rimmed in red from crying. "When Fergus gets here, ye will see! He will get her back for me! And he will kill all of ye!"

Rodrick took a tentative step forward, the bag with Fergus's head dangling from one hand. "Fergus is no' comin' back."

"Ye lie!" she screamed. "He is on his way here now. But first, he is goin' to kill yer whore of a wife. Ye will see! Then he and I will raise Burunild together."

Rodrick shook his head in disgust. The woman was just as mad as Fergus. Anthara was just as culpable as her husband in what had happened to Muriel. Anthara had refused to listen to Muriel's plea for help. Instead of helping her, she sided with Fergus. She'd even gone so far as to help in some of the beatings Muriel had received. Nay, he would not feel an ounce of remorse or pity for this woman.

"Fergus is no' comin' back," he repeated. "No' today, no' tomorrow, no' ever."

He could see she was not quite ready yet to believe him. Cautiously, she took a step back, her eyes darting around the room for something else to throw at them. "Ye lie," she said. This time, she did not scream. Rodrick could see her resolve was beginning to fade.

Rodrick slowly lifted the sack containing Fergus's head. "Nay, I do no' lie to ye," he replied. He tossed the sack onto a chair, where it landed with a hard thud. "Ye can have that," he said, "or give it to his father. Either way, I do no' care." He turned to leave but stopped himself. "Ye can tell the bloody bastard who fathered yer husband that if I ever I see him or his men or kin anywhere near me wife or daughter, I shall do the same to them." He nodded toward the sack once before leaving.

As he and Callum crossed over the threshold and back into the late afternoon air, they heard the plaintive wail of the newly widowed Anthara MacDonald. Neither man looked back.

CHAPTER TWENTY-ONE

With his wife and daughter wrapped protectively in his arms, Rodrick began the long journey home. Just as they'd done the previous spring, they rode fast and hard. Neither Rodrick nor Ian knew if Walter MacDonald would declare war over the taking of his son's life.

By the time they reached the Mackintosh and McLaren keep, Muriel was beyond exhausted. Road worn and weary, Rodrick carried her and Cora into their little home. With Rose and Deidre's help, Muriel bathed in a tub of hot water before slipping into a nightdress and into bed. With Muriel in their good hands, Rodrick went with the rest of the men to bathe in the loch.

Rodrick and Muriel had said very little to one another during the ride home. He supposed 'twas exhaustion — both in mind and body — that kept her from speaking much. She'd watched as her husband had taken the life of her tormentor and abuser. He reckoned it might take a few days for her to come to grips with everything that had happened.

At least that was his hope. In truth, he worried his sweet wife would now be terrified of him. She had, after all, watched him slice Fergus's throat and cut his head from his body. Mayhap she would now think him naught more than a vicious murderer. Even though she *had* asked him, nay *told* him to kill Fergus, it could have been something said in the heat of the moment. She might not have truly meant it. And she certainly didn't need to watch as he did it.

Mayhap he should have ordered her removed before he killed him.

Mayhap he should have simply ridden off with her and dealt with Fergus later.

Some men might have left their wives alone to sort out their feelings. Some men might have kept their own worries and feelings unto themselves. But Rodrick worried that ignoring anything at this point would put a wedge betwixt him and his wife. Nay, he decided, 'twas best to deal with everything now. Like a gangrenous wound if left alone and uncared for far too long, it would grow and fester until 'twas deadly.

Upon returning to their home and finding Muriel and Cora fast asleep, he slipped out of his clothes, into his braes, and slid into the bed. Muriel was facing him, with Cora bundled and sleeping in the crook of her arm. They looked so peaceful as they slept. *On the morrow,* he decided. *On the morrow, after a good night's sleep, we will talk.*

Muriel opened her eyes as he pulled the warm fur up to cover her shoulder.

"Ye smell good," she said sleepily.

Certainly, a woman terrified of her husband wouldn't comment on such a thing, would she?

"Thank ye, Rodrick," she said, her voice naught but a whisper. Reaching out, she placed a warm hand on his cheek. "Thank ye for comin' for us."

Relief was slow to build. "Did ye think I would no'?"

She smiled warmly. "I knew in me heart the only thing that would stop ye would be yer own death."

He took her hand in his and kissed her palm. "And ye would be right." He was relieved and quite glad that she didn't pull her hand away.

"Rodrick, I want to tell ye somethin'," she whispered.

Dread and worry reared their ugly heads. Had Fergus hurt her again? Was she about to tell him of her ordeal, of something ugly and sordid? He willed his nerves to settle and took in a deep, fortifying breath.

"I love ye, Rodrick MacElroy. With all me heart."

He could not have been more stunned had she hit him over the head with a battle-axe. Uncertain if he'd heard her correctly, he said, "What?"

"I love ye," she repeated. "And no' just because ye came fer us. I realized it no' long after ye left to go after the Randalls."

All at once, he felt enveloped in a sense of warmth and peace. 'Twas as comforting as a heavy fur in wintertime. Like the heat from a brazier on a cold day. But so much more than that.

"I missed ye," she went on to say. "So much so that 'twas a physical ache. I knew then that I could no' miss ye as much if I did no' love ye."

For the first time in his adult life, Rodrick the Bold's eyes grew damp. He felt no shame in it. Nay, he felt naught but elation, pride, and utter joy. "I love ye, Muriel. With all that I am, I love ye."

Her smile burned bright, her eyes filled with happiness and love. "I ken," she told him. "I've kent for some time now. And I be verra glad that ye do."

He kissed her palm again before placing it on his chest, just over his heart. "Ye have made me verra happy this day, lass. Verra happy."

They talked then, for the next hour or so. First, they discussed all that had transpired over the last few days. Nay, Muriel did not hold him in any kind of low regard over killing Fergus. Just the opposite. She was grateful. Although she did admit she didn't truly enjoy *watching* it.

Just as the embers in the brazier began to die down, Rodrick the Bold and his wife fell asleep, holding each other's hands.

It may have taken three decades, but his Christmas Tide wish had finally come true. Rodrick the Bold finally had a wife and child. He had so much more than that.

He had his family.

CHAPTER TWENTY-TWO

R odrick was the first to rise the following morning. He left his wife and babe to sleep as he dressed quietly and started the fire.

A new day had dawned, a new beginning for him and Muriel. A day in which he knew, unequivocally, that his wife *loved* him. Loved him like a wife loved a husband, in a romantic fashion, and not as one would love a brother, father, or friend. She proved that to him last night, after she put Cora in her cradle. She spent the next two hours *showing* him just how much she loved him and how ready she was to move on.

While he would have loved nothing more than to wile away the day, staying abed with his wife and making silly faces just to see his daughter smile, there was much to be done. First, he needed to meet with Ian. There was still the matter of the Randall raid that needed to be dealt with. He also wanted to thank Ian for helping him to get Muriel and Cora back.

When he stepped out of his home, he was met with brilliant sunshine, birds flittering about, and the sound of his clan coming to life. *I could die right now, and die a most happy man,* he mused.

One of the women folk was walking by, pulling him from his quiet reverie. She bore the oddest expression when she looked at him. As if he were some deranged madman. 'Twas then he realized he was smiling. He supposed no one was accustomed to seeing his lips curved upward, unless he was in battle or training his men.

"Good day to ye," he said with a nod. *Let them think me mad,* he thought to himself. *'Twill keep them off balance.*

The woman said nothing, but she did pick up her pace.

Taking the path that led to the keep, he continued to smile. *Aye, life is good,* he thought.

That was until he saw Ian coming toward him.

Ian did not look happy.

Before Rodrick could inquire as to what was making his chief look mad enough to bite nails, Ian said, "*Ye* have a visitor."

Confused as to why a visitor would cause his chief to be so angry, Rodrick stopped and asked, "Who?"

With his nostrils flared, Ian let out an angry breath. "Walter MacDonald."

RODRICK, IAN, AND TEN OF THEIR MEN RODE OUT OF THE KEEP TO MEET with Walter MacDonald. Ian was furious. Before mounting his horse moments before, he said, "I shall give ye over to the MacDonald before I enter into a war."

From his expression, Rodrick did not doubt him for a moment.

Walter MacDonald sat tall in his saddle. Though he might have been nearing sixty, he was still a formidable looking man.

Leaving the rest of the men a few paces behind, Ian and Rodrick rode out to meet the chief of Clan MacDonald. The father of the man Rodrick had killed just a few days ago.

"Which one of ye be the one called Rodrick the Bold?" Walter asked. His voice boomed and echoed over the open landscape.

"I be Rodrick the Bold," Rodrick replied dryly.

Walter studied him closely for a brief moment. "Ye be the one who killed me son?"

"Aye, I am," Rodrick answered. He tried his best to keep the pride he felt in doing so out of his voice.

The MacDonald shifted slightly in the saddle as he continued his close scrutinization. Rodrick and Ian maintained their air of indifference.

"I have kent fer some time that the day would come when an angry husband, father or brother would kill him," Walter said. "Or some young lass who had finally had enough."

Rodrick continued his stone-cold silence. He knew he could learn more by listening than by talking. And they needed to know why the MacDonald was here. The wrong word said now could lead to dire consequences.

"Fergus," Walter began as he shifted his weight once again, "was no' me best work. He was a fool and a deviant, that I will no' deny."

Rodrick kept his opinion on the matter to himself. However, Ian finally broke his silence. "Have ye come to declare war to avenge the death of yer son?"

Rodrick knew they could ill afford a war at the moment. Ian had to be worried, but no one else would have guessed. His tone was that of a calm and unconcerned man.

Walter raised one bushy brow in surprise right before chuckling. "Ye be Ian Mackintosh, aye?"

"I am," Ian replied.

"Ye can put yer worries aside. I am no' here to declare war."

"Then why are ye here?" Ian asked.

"I've come to thank the man who finally had the guts to take me son's life."

Rodrick and Ian glanced at one another, but their expressions belied what they were both truly thinking.

"I ken it sounds cruel that a father would think so poorly of a son," Walter told them. "But as I said, Fergus was no' me best work."

Rodrick couldn't fathom having a son he would not grieve or mourn for. He had to give Walter MacDonald some credit for realizing his son was a demented and deviant individual. However, Rodrick had to believe that he would have done everything in his power to help any of his children off the beaten path and onto the path of righteousness and good.

As if Walter could read his mind, he said, "I did everything I could fer him."

The three men sat quietly for a long while. Two were trying to gauge the truthfulness and sincerity of the one.

"Rodrick the Bold," Walter said, breaking the lengthy silence, "I would like to speak to ye alone."

Rodrick and Ian sat a bit taller, uncertain if this was for nefarious purposes to get Rodrick alone.

"I want to speak to ye about the child."

RODRICK THOUGHT LONG AND HARD BEFORE MAKING HIS DECISION. Cora had been claimed as Fergus MacDonald's child and Walter MacDonald's grandchild. By law, Walter had more rights over Cora than either Muriel or Rodrick. Pushing his worries aside, he finally agreed.

The two men dismounted and walked side by side toward the creek. Tension roped around Rodrick's shoulders, his senses on high alert for any sign of treachery. Knowing Ian and the others had his back did give him a better sense of strength.

"As ye ken," Walter began as he clasped his hands behind his back, "I did declare the child as me grandchild. Publicly and for all the world to ken."

Aye, Rodrick knew it because he'd witnessed it first-hand. "If ye think we will give Cora over to ye—" he began.

"Nay," Walter interrupted. "That is no' what I want. The mother seems to love her child verra much. I believe she be in good care here."

Rodrick nodded his agreement but otherwise remained quiet.

"Me son's inheritance, by rights, belongs to the child."

"Her name is Cora," Rodrick told him. "Cora MacElroy."

Walter stopped their forward progression and turned to face Rodrick. "The inheritance belongs to her," he said, ignoring Rodrick's declaration. Tugging at something draped into his belt, Walter retrieved a hefty pouch. He tried handing it to Rodrick, but he refused to take it.

"Do no' let yer pride stand in the way of yer daughter havin' what is rightfully hers."

Walter's words *yer daughter* did not go unnoticed. "I can raise her on me own. We do no' need yer help."

Walter rolled his eyes. "Ye be as stubborn as I," he said. "'Tis no' fer ye to use to raise her. 'Tis fer ye to give to her when she reaches an appropriate age. Or to give to her as a dowry."

Rodrick stared at the offered pouch for a long moment. From its size, he could reckon it contained a good deal of money. None of this made a bit of sense. He was talking to the father of the man he'd just killed. A man who could have started a war. A man who could take Cora and naught could be legally done to stop it.

Yet instead of declaring war or seeking retribution on behalf of his son or demanding custody of Cora, Walter MacDonald was being congenial. "What do ye get from all this?" Rodrick asked. He knew there had to be more to his generosity that merely that of a loving —if that could even be said — grandfather.

"I want naught but two things from ye," Walter began.

Rodrick was suspicious but tried to keep an open mind.

"I want *yer* word," he said, pointing a thick index finger at him, "that ye will raise Cora better than I raised Fergus."

That would be as easy as breathing, Rodrick thought. "And?"

"And," Walter said. Rodrick could see him struggling ever so slightly to find the right words. "I would like to see the girl child at least once a year." He stopped Rodrick's protests with a raised hand. "She need no' ken I be her grandsire," he said. "I merely want to make certain ye be keepin' the first promise. It can be at a time and place of yer choosin'."

Rodrick did not think it necessarily a horrible request. "Me wife will never agree to such," he told him.

"Need she ken?" Walter asked, suggesting he lie.

"Of course she needs to ken!" Rodrick exclaimed. "I will no' keep such a thing from her."

Walter thought on it for a long moment. "So ye will tell her about the inheritance and our meetin'? What if she refuses all the gold in that pouch?"

Gold? Rodrick looked at the fat, heavy pouch. He thought, at best, it might be naught more than a few pieces of silver. But gold?

"Will *ye* be able to give a dowry such as this to her? To any of yer children?"

Rodrick need not answer, for they both knew he couldn't.

"If ye allow me to see Cora once a year, I will see to it that all of yer children, born or to be born, each receives the same amount of coin fer either a dowry or whatever they wish."

There was no way he could offer anything even remotely similar to Cora. And if last night was any indication of his future, he and Muriel would be having many, many children. Could he, in good conscience, keep such a secret from Muriel? She was bound to find out sooner or later. Especially when he presented a heavy bag of gold as dowry or marital gift.

He supposed, for a moment, that he could take the money and put it away for safe-keeping. Later, mayhap a decade from now, he could tell Muriel. Aye, she might be mad enough to bludgeon him to death with a cooking pot, but at least his children would be cared for.

Realizing he was not a young man anymore, and realizing he could never give any of his children such a gift on his own, he made a decision to accept.

Rodrick could only hope and pray he could convince his wife of the soundness of his plan.

EPILOGUE

'T would be nearly two decades before Rodrick confessed to Muriel his arrangement with Walter MacDonald. While some might have called it an act of cowardice to keep such a thing secret, Rodrick stood firm on his decision. Too much harm had been done to his wife at the hands of the mad man that was Fergus MacDonald. As far as Rodrick was concerned, taking the man's life and his father's offered gold was not nearly enough recompense.

So, kept it a secret he did until his beautiful daughter Cora reached the age of seven and ten. Rodrick would have kept the secret longer had the poor girl not fallen in love with a Mackintosh man. And had that man not been one of good character, honor—a young man Rodrick had known since the day he was born—he would have gainsaid the match. As much as he would have preferred all four of his daughters to be sent to a convent the moment they discovered the lads, Muriel was adamantly opposed. Besides, who could say no to a match betwixt their first born and the son of a clan chief? Nay, he could find no good reason not to allow Cora to wed James Mackintosh.

When he finally confessed to Muriel the nearly two-decade-long secret, she was not nearly as angry had he imagined she would be.

"I've known about yer little agreement with Walter for years," she told him on the day of Cora's wedding. Apparently, Cora was not as good at keeping a secret at Rodrick. When Cora had turned eight, she had told her mother all about Walter MacDonald. "I figured ye would eventually tell me," Muriel said with a knowing smile. "But if ye ever think to keep another secret such as that from me, I shall no' wait for ye to fall asleep to kill ye. I shall do it so that ye can look me in the eye and watch."

There was no doubt to the sincerity in her voice, nor her abilities. He had not only trained her in the use of knives, dirks, and *sgian dubs,* over the years, he had taught her the proper use of swords as well. He held on to the belief that she loved him too much to kill him. But he wasn't about to take any chances.

Rodrick had also trained each of his daughters and his only son just as diligently as he'd trained their mother. No man could be prouder of his wife and children than Rodrick the bold. He had a most perfect life. One he was quite content with.

For years, he lived his life most honorably and proudly, with a sense of contentment he would not have thought possible before meeting Muriel. He would be nearly seventy-years old before that sense of contentment would be tested beyond anything he had ever previously experienced.

The God-awful dream — of the red-haired beauty with eyes the color of emeralds — returned to him, and with unparalleled vengeance. Many years ago, he had believed the lass was Muriel, but his wife looked nothing at all like the image that had haunted him. Years had passed by without the recurring dream.

He had forgotten all about the beautiful creature, forgotten her torment and lamentation. He had forgotten all about her and the sickening sensation the nightly visits had left behind.

Now, the sweet lass was back, calling to him, through the abyss, through a mist so thick he believed it would strangle him. She was begging for his help, so desperate and disconsolate he could feel it to his very marrow.

Soaked in sweat, his old heart beating violently against his chest, he woke crying out her name.

"Isobella!"

He now knew who the red-haired beauty who had called to him decades ago was. 'Twas his second born daughter, Isobella.

And she needed him.

AFTERWORD FROM SUZAN

I truly enjoyed writing this story. Some of you might think that I ended it on a cliff hanger. To a certain extent, that is true! However, I firmly believe that where one story ends another begins.

There are times, while writing a story, that an image pops into your mind as vividly and as real as the next breath you take. And that was true with this story.

While writing *Rodrick the Bold*, I kept thinking about the image of the red-haired beauty with the emerald green eyes. For the life of me, I didn't know and couldn't understand the importance of her and that image, only that she *was* important. I could feel it in my gut. It wasn't until I sat down to write the epilogue that I began to understand.

Yes, I will be writing a story for Isobella, the lovely daughter of Rodrick and Muriel. I just don't know *when*. But I do promise you, that rattling around somewhere in the deep recesses of my mind, her story does exist. Right now, it's just bits and pieces and fleeting images.

As has happened with a few of my other books—*McKenna's Honor* comes to mind—that story came to me early one morning, whilst I was tending to my morning ablutions. From out of no where came one sentence: *Angus hangs at dawn.* Wham! Like that, the images came pouring in, and for a brief moment I thought I had lost my mind. I wrote *McKenna's Honor* in three weeks.

I know that one day, Isobella's story will come to me in nearly full form, just like *McKenna's Honor* did.

With much love and gratitude,

Suzan Tisdale
 Author. Storyteller. Cheeky Wench.

ABOUT THE AUTHOR

USA Today Bestselling Author, storyteller and cheeky wench, SUZAN TISDALE lives in the Midwest with her verra handsome carpenter husband. All but one of her children have left the nest. Her pets consist of dust bunnies and a dozen poodle-sized, backyard-dwelling groundhogs – all of which run as free and unrestrained as the voices in her head. And she doesn't own a single pair of yoga pants, much to the shock and horror of her fellow authors. She prefers to write in her pajamas.

Suzan writes Scottish historical romance/fiction, with honorable and perfectly imperfect heroes and strong, feisty heroines. And bad guys she kills off in delightfully wicked ways.

She published her first novel, Laiden's Daughter, in December, 2011, as a gift for her mother. That one book started a journey which has led to fifteen published titles, with two more being released in the spring of 2017. To date, she has sold more than 350,000 copies of her books around the world. They have been translated into four foreign languages (Italian, French, German, and Spanish.)

You will find her books in digital, paperback, and audiobook formats.

Get text messages on new releases!
Text CheekyWenchUS to 24587

Stay Up To Date
www.suzantisdale.com

Email: suzan@suzantisdale.com

Tap any of the icons below to follow me at Facebook, Twitter, Goodreads, Pinterest, and Amazon.

ALSO BY SUZAN TISDALE

The Clan MacDougall Series

Laiden's Daughter

Findley's Lass

Wee William's Woman

McKenna's Honor

The Clan Graham Series

Rowan's Lady

Frederick's Queen

The Mackintoshes and McLarens Series

Ian's Rose

The Bowie Bride

Brogan's Promise

The Clan McDunnah Series

A Murmur of Providence

A Whisper of Fate

A Breath of Promise

Moirra's Heart Series

Stealing Moirra's Heart

Saving Moirra's Heart

Stand Alone Novels

Isle of the Blessed

Made in the USA
Middletown, DE
10 March 2018